Dedications

To my imagination,
You finally got your wish, freedom.

To my mother,
You're the best, I am nothing without you.

To my brother and sister,
Live your dreams! You were meant to be great. To
me, you already are.

To my best friend,
Thank you for being my fact checker, you know
what I mean!

BOUND TO YOU

Table of Contents

This is a work of fiction.

Names, characters, places, and incidents either are the product of the author's imagination or are used fictitiously. Any resemblance to actual persons, living or dead, events, or locales are entirely coincidental.

In the beginning...

"Good morning, Mrs. Preston, what can I do for you?" The owner of the art boutique asked. "Kamari, it is wonderful to see you this morning! My word, I wish you would start selling those paintings of that magnificent wolf. It is simply breathtaking and would look amazing in my den. I am certain Mr. Preston would agree."

Kamari Lee smiled fondly at her loyal customer, Mrs. Preston. She was a huge fan of her artwork, she always told her that her artwork rivaled those that hung in the Louvre or the MET.

The Preston's were a wealthy elder couple who decided to settle in the sleepy town of Lovingshire (low-veng-shire). Mr. Preston had retired after being a stockbroker for 35 years and Mrs. Preston was a homemaker and an avid gardener once their four children were out of the house.

"I would, but there's such a strong emotional connection. If I part with it, I feel my heartstrings tear a bit, I can't... it's too near and dear to my heart." She fawns over her latest interpretation of her white wolf. Standing on the cliff from Destiny Falls, the wolf is howling to the full moon. His coat is snow-white with one exception, not a flaw because she thought it made it look unique, a black spot circling its left eye, it was the opposite to the magnificent white fur, it resembled a dalmatian's spot.

"Well, dear, we can't have that, now can we? So, let's talk about my newest ask for Parker's office. He has a blank wall that is in dire need of your touch." Kamari chuckles and takes a pad and pen to scribble down her ideas.

A sudden bang at his private study knocks Kayden out of his peaceful frame of mind. He sighs bitterly, "Can't I have 30 minutes to myself?!" He runs his hands down his face trying not to turn any shade of red that annotated just how angry he was. He walks through the secret door and shuts it behind him, walking through his office he yanks the door and lets it slam against the wall.

"What?!" Suddenly he is met by two eyes that did not stand for his attitude, he changes his demeanor quickly. "I'm sorry, mom."

She pokes her finger into his chest. "I know you are not yelling at the very woman who gave you life and raised you to be the leader of this great pack, right Kayden James Miller?"

He sighs, "No, mom..."

She continues, "And I know that you wouldn't be screaming at the only woman in your life right now...lose me and you'll be alone."

He rolls his eyes. "Mom, please, not this again."

He walks to his chair at his desk and sits down. His mother was 5' 3" of black cat firecracker. She never minced words with her only son, she wanted what she wanted, his happiness, for him to find his mate and fall in love. She sits on the edge of the desk holding his face in her hand.

"Son, I only want the best for you. Your father and I are getting up in age and you will be the Alpha leader of this pack, but I don't need that to be your entire life. I need grand babies, Kayden."

There it was, the ulterior motive. He sighs violently, almost ripping his lungs from their stem.

"Don't you know I know that, mom? What I wouldn't do to have my mate, but I just haven't found her. She's close I can almost feel her but she's just out of my reach, all I can do is keep searching but until then, my pack comes first."

She looked at the heartbreak in his emerald green eyes, she didn't want to be too hard on him when he was only 25, and she knew that watching his friends, family, and even his own leadership find their mates was heart-wrenching. She sighs and kisses her boy on the forehead.

"Okay, dear, I won't keep you from your work. Will you attend Alpha Martin's ball next week?"

He knew that was a plea to attend with the luck of finding his mate. He didn't want to fight with her.

"Of course, mom, I'll be there." He plasters on the brightest, most fake smile to please her.

When she steps out, Evan steps in. "Hey, what did she want?" Kayden pulls the book to open the door to his secret room and Evan follows.

Only a handful knew about his room, he needed an outlet from the chaos that is being a pack leader.

"The usual, she wants me to parade around at Alpha Martin's ball in hopes I find my mate."

He sits down in front of his latest work. It was a statuesque beautiful woman with curly black hair that grazed her shoulder gazing at Destiny Falls. You could only see the back of her, none of her features but to him, she was absolutely perfect.

Evan walks closer to it. "Wow, this one is beautiful. You always draw her from behind or her face is obscured, why is that?"

Kayden picks up his brush to add a few strokes to the ivory-colored dress flowing in the wind. "I only see her in my dreams and when she turns around, I always wake up."

He sighs as he drops the brush into the cup to clean. He picks up a super fine brush to bring out the movement in her hair. "I always hope one day that I stay long enough to see her but..." He trails off and sighs once more.

No further words exchanged between them, Evan knows exactly how he feels without another syllable. He was his best friend since they were 12 and his second in command. He hoped that his buddy would find his mate like he did two years and two pups ago. "Don't worry about it, she's out there you will meet in due time."

The Bestie

The door chimes, signaling a customer.

"Kammi Bear!"

She knew that voice anywhere, it belonged to her best friend, Vanessa. She saunters in and takes a seat on the stool behind the counter and grins.

"What is the plan for this glorious Friday night?" She smiles her Cheshire grin, hinting her free spirit wanting to let loose.

"No, Nessa I have a new set of commissions from Mrs. Preston and I need to finish up on this painting." She points to her white wolf.

"I don't get it Kam, why are you constantly drawing that thing? Then you don't sell any, what is the point?"

Kamari glances over the details of her next work of art and then smiles when she gazes at her wolf.

"It's my muse, I don't know Nessa, I just feel so much emotion when I paint it. I can't get it out of my head and frankly, I don't want to. There's something there I can't explain." She lovingly looks at her almost finished piece.

Nessa clears her throat and Kam's attention focuses back on her clearly uninterested friend.

"You. need. to. get. out. Let's just go to Jack's for a few hours and celebrate your sales." She knew she was using it as an excuse to get her out of her comfort zone.

"Whyyyy?! It's the same people at the bar every night, this isn't New York, Lovingshire consists of 500 people and I don't want to see that jackass John nor his buddies get drunk then play how-hard-can-I-ram-my-head-into-this-wall and let's not forget that I hate his guts." She sighs while jotting down notes from her previous conversation with Mrs. Preston.

Seeing as she was going to get nowhere, she offers another solution.

"Okay, you're right. How about a trip to the movies to see the new Aquaman, I mean...Jason Momoa...we need to see him half-naked and dripping wet."

She swoons as she licks her lips and bumps her shoulder against her.

"Well, he is sex on a stick so sure, why not." Vanessa squeals in excitement then looks at the time.

"Oh, we need to go soon, it starts in 45 minutes and you need to change...please."

Kamari looks down at her paint-stained clothing, she has a point.

"Let's go to my place."

She takes a short moment to glance at her wolf, she had never felt such a strong connection, it was odd, but she relished in how she felt. She turns off the lights and locks up for the night.

Kayden loved the freedom of running around his territory, it included the beauty that was Destiny Falls but it was open to the public separating his territory so everyone could also enjoy its beauty. He hopped the fence near the edge of the beautiful lookout point. He shakes his fur and lies on the ground watching the water trickle over the rocks and down the stream.

Phoenix: Hey, hey, hey...she's close Kayden, I feel her!

Kayden's wolf, Phoenix yelps, he's hopping around like a five-year-old on an endless supply of sugar. He doesn't respond excitedly because he knew that he just had no energy. He wanted their meeting to be natural, not forced.

Kayden: I know buddy, I know. We will find her, in due time.

It's not that he didn't want to find his mate, it's the way that some of the mates found each other that made him want to do this right. I mean, ramming your tongue down your newly found mate's throat in the middle of training, or the group dinner, or during a gala was not his ideal meeting and was very cringe worthy.

Though he portrayed himself as a strong and aggressive Alpha male he still yearned for his Luna, the side that would bring out his compassion and love. He knew he had to emit masculinity and strength and never show signs of weakness but still...he couldn't deny he wanted to be loved, to be in love.

After some time observing the falls, he heads back to the pack house. He shifts near a tree where he hid a pair of basketball shorts that hang off his 6' 4" frame, sweat pouring as he wipes with his forearm to avoid getting into his eyes. He runs into his third in command, Miles who was barking orders to adhere to for the rest of the night. They nod at each other as he goes into the house and up towards his wing of the estate.

The grounds were huge, the pack house was three stories and permanently housed the Alpha, second, third, and fourth in command. Each gets a wing of the home with Kayden occupying the entire third floor including his office. Included on the compound was an Olympic size pool, sauna, state of the art training facility, medical house, and horse stables. It also had a day care facility and nursing home for the aging elders.

He uses his shaky legs to climb the stairs to his floor, he passes near a closed door, and he takes a deep breath before opening, almost as if he was gaining his composure. With a click of a lock, he was staring at a beautifully decorated nursery, rich in dark and light grays, black and lilac. Beautifully decorated to resemble the moonlight sky dotted with thousands of stars. The crib, adorned with light gray lace cascading from the ceiling, was a beautiful centerpiece to the room that had everything new parents would need for their pup. When the time would come, he would unveil this to his love, but right now it was a tough reality as he slowly closed the door.

Leaning against the shower wall, he watches the water cascade off his body while he fantasizes about the unknown angel haunting his dreams and his artwork. Every time he dreamed of her his heart would be full as she took his hand leading him to the falls. He felt complete in his dreams, she radiated love and he basked in it. He would find her...and she would be his.

Decisions Decisions

The next morning was more chaotic for Kayden than usual, everyone wanted approval for various requests, and it was becoming too much. He grunts out frustratingly, pushing his desk forward a few feet in anger, knocking all items to the floor and the room goes deathly quiet.

"Why can't this be handled at the lowest level, why am I stuck making all these trivial decisions?! If I didn't trust you, I wouldn't have put you all in my command! So, this is how it will go, Miles will handle the dungeon and rogues, Brent will handle all security details and border patrol and Evan will deal with contracts and negotiations between packs. I will handle all business directly to do with the other Alphas. Dismissed..."

He doesn't utter another word as he spins his chair to the bay window, Evan stays back. Kayden sighs knowing he's still in the room.

"What, Evan?!"

He doesn't bother turning around. Evan tilts his head at the back of his best friend's chair, his silence speaks volumes. Eventually, he spins his chair around. "I'm sorry, I'm just so unbelievably stressed out, I just need you guys to pick up your part of the work. We have a lot of people to protect."

Alpha, Beta, there were rogues spotted near our northern border.

They both sigh.

Contact Miles and Brent, I designated them for this, thank you.

As he cuts off the mind link with the border patrol, he links Evan.

Let's see how they fare, link me if you need me, I'm going to my haven.

He pulls the book to open his room, his sanctuary, looking back once more.

"If you capture them don't kill them immediately, see what information we can get out of them first...give them 48 hours then kill them." Evan nods.

Kamari puts the keys into the lock to start another day at her studio. She loved the smell of paint in the morning. She flips the light switch and opens the blinds. Sitting down to enjoy her bagel and coffee she smiles at her painting, she loved it so. "Maybe next time I'll draw you as I would view you from my balcony. Maybe I should name you...hmm, Patches? Spot? No, those are dumb and unoriginal. You look like a magical, mystical creature. I'm sure that spot is rare and special. I know, Phoenix, that's it, suits you perfectly." She smiles, happy with her name choice. As she sips her coffee, a young gentleman strolls in.

He simply nods as he admires her work around the studio. She couldn't help but notice how rugged he was, he was around six-foot, nicely built, she could tell by his bulging forearms, and a butt that could sell a pair of Levi's to the blind. He had dark semi curly hair and sea-foam green eyes. He turns to her and she feels a rush of heat throughout her body, he is gorgeous. He walks up to her counter flashing a million-dollar smile.

"Well, good morning, gorgeous I hear you are the one to come to for beautiful artwork."

She can feel the blush in her cheek hoping he doesn't notice.

"Depends on who sent you." She smirks and he chuckles.

"Well, I just moved here and ran into a girl named Vanessa at the diner and she told me that if I need to decorate my place to see what you have to offer. By the way, my name is Cole." She takes his hand.

"Kamari, but my friends call me Kam as you have already met my best friend, obviously. Well, are you looking for anything in particular?" She ogles him as he turns away from her to view her collection.

"There are so many beautiful pieces, especially that gorgeous white wolf. That's the most detailed one I've ever seen. Are you selling that particular piece?" He points to the white wolf running through the forest under the moonlight. Noticing there was no price tag.

She sighs. "Unfortunately, all the wolf paintings are not for sale. They are like my children and I can't part with them yet, sorry."

He looks back and smiles. "No need to apologize, I wouldn't want to either. Anyway, I do love this portrait and this abstract. Yes...I do believe Brian will love both pieces."

She perks up. "Oh, is he your brother or roommate?" He spins around flashing that swoon-worthy smile.

"Oh, my boyfriend."

*Of course...*she sighs both internally and externally putting on a fake smile as she comes from behind the counter.

"Well, I'm sure he will love them, I'll even knock off 10% since you bought more than one." He nods as he reaches for his wallet. After their transaction he gets her personal info so they could all hang out. He wanted the grand tour of all that was Lovingshire, that was probably a ten-minute tour of this sleepy haven.

Twenty minutes later Vanessa strolls in before her 2nd shift at work. "So, you get any...new business?" Her break in wording was super cheeky, so very Nessa. She stares at her momentarily.

"Why, yes I did. I was met by this beautiful stranger with a megawatt smile who strolled in looking for some art...for he and his boyfriend's new apartment."

Vanessa's face falls as her words shattered her hope. "Damn it! I was so certain he was perfect for you or at least a good f-"

"Nessa!"

She couldn't hide her embarrassment if she tried. It had been some time since her last tryst, with John, surprisingly.

What?!

Besides his childish antics he was amazing in bed...and that's it. He had no communication or relationship skills whatsoever and always spent his free time drinking with his friends who held the same lack of skills but weren't as handsome as John.

John stood 6' 2" of rippling muscle, blonde hair swept to the side, permanent after sex hair and piercing ocean blue eyes. He would toss her over his shoulder when he came over to ravish her and damn was he good at it.

Suddenly, Nessa interrupts her by snapping her fingers rapidly. "Sex flashbacks? I mean John is always there as an...outlet, I'm sure he wouldn't mind. Maybe you should hit him up? Nothing wrong with casual sex. Besides, there are only a handful of hot guys here." She shrugs but before giving it a second thought Kam shakes her head.

"I'm not trying to sleep down the roster, Nessa. I want that typical love story and I'm not willing to settle for less."

She glances over at her unfinished work. She gathers her supplies and starts with short strokes to emphasize the movement in the picture.

"Well, you're not but I am. I got myself a date with Jared tonight and if all goes well, I'll be screaming his name by 2am. You should come by..." She almost makes a mis-stroke where she doesn't want it as she spins back around.

"Why the hell would I do that?"

Nessa shrugs as she heads towards the doors.

"It's one way to get off, I'm just saying." Kam just shakes her head.

"I'm just fine, Nessa, enjoy your hookup." Nessa winks before she leaves. "Oh, I definitely plan on it." With that, she's out the door.

Her best friend's words stung a bit with the truth. She wasn't a casual hookup kind of girl, she even thought she and John had a fighting chance before she caught him balls deep in some girl's mouth at a house party.

Well, she wasn't just some girl, for some reason Bridget had it out for Kam but Kam didn't care enough about her to find out why.

Kam wasn't even visibly upset about catching them but emotionally, she was a wreck... she and John

were in a casual relationship even though she wanted more. She was super disappointed in him and never spoke to him again, even after the atypical apology and flowers outside her business, her doorstep and even her car. She never reacted and never looked him in the eye again.
She wouldn't give him the satisfaction and he finally admitted defeat but that did not stop him from gazing at her when their paths did cross. He knew he lost a good thing.

Everybody Loves John Michael

Suddenly, as if his ears were burning, John walks in. She gasps and drops her brush.

"John..."

She stands up but looks down, she still didn't want to look him in the eye. He was on a mission as he walked towards her with purpose, grabbing her chin to tilt it up. She couldn't hide the hurt on her face, the tears threatening to flow over the wall she built. She felt the cold lump in her throat, and she stared into his eyes, they flickered causing her to get lost in them.

He rubs his hand on his neck. "Hey Kam, it's really good to see you."

That's it?

She thought as she scoffed. She nods slowly and backs away.

"Wow, John, that's all you could come up with, typical. What do you want? Why are you even here?" She stands behind the counter as he tries to pick his face off the ground.

"Kam, I-I don't know what to say even after all this time. You look so beautifully breathtaking. It wasn't long ago that you were mine and we were happy together..."

She huffs "And don't forget the part where you royally f--screwed up and broke my heart, John. You allowed what took place to happen at Aaron's party, for all to see, and they did, John! They did and when you were caught, she had a smirk proving she could take whoever she wanted and she did, she took you from me and I looked like a fool. I spent days, weeks sulking and heartbroken."

She let the tears flow, it had built up and finally the dam burst. He steps forward but she steps back.

"Just stop...what do you really want, John Michael?" She only called him that when she wanted him to get to the point. He started fidgeting, anxious to get to the reason he was standing before her. He takes a deep breath.

"I- I would like for you to paint my engagement photo. You're the best artist in town and I know I screwed up badly with you, but I wouldn't want to go to anyone else. You're an amazing talent and I know I am asking for a lot, but I want to apologize, Kam, I didn't mean for this to happen like this. You deserve a man who can love you with every fiber of his being and I just wasn't that guy, I was, I am a total screw up."

Her face is pale and void of all emotion. The color draining from her tightly squeezed hand.

"Who is it?"

He tilts his head in question.

"Who the fuck is she, John?!"

He jumps at her reaction.

"It's...Bridget. Our families arranged it thinking this union is what's best for both of us. They want the portrait to hang in their family room."

She turns away from him, the tears flow tremendously, her chest heaves in anger. Luckily at that moment Nessa comes in. She stops in her tracks when she sees John's shaky demeanor. She doesn't say anything, she is here to back her best friend and, if need be, give him a piece of her mind.

Kam turns back around, and her face riddled in tears. "Huh...are you kidding me? This has to be a joke; it just has to be. Did you really think I would be okay with painting your engagement photo with the whore who stole you from me?! You can't think I would take such a ridiculous offer...get the fuck out, John! I hope you two are very miserable together, don't ever look in my direction ever again, you are dead to me! A bit of parting advice...you better keep her on a fucking leash, I will not hesitate to undo all her precious plastic surgery. She may have won but the prize was obviously...*lacking*." She eyes him up and down viciously.

Her last words were so calm and emotionless, but they ripped his heart to shreds. With her final stare he jerks back, tears falling.

"I-I'm s-sorry Kam, I didn't deserve you. I hope you find happiness; I do."

With that he leaves her shop. Kam slides down the wall and has a complete breakdown. Nessa locks the door and displays the closed sign. She holds her close and lets her cry all over her silk shirt.

"Shhh, now. You said what you had to say and it's over now. I know you don't want to hear this right now, but I am so proud of you. You gave that bastard everything you've felt and then some. He deserved to feel your pain." For the next twenty minutes Nessa hums as Kam lies in self-pity.

Did he really think that was a suitable ask? To ask your ex to paint you and your bimbo? She truly wanted the worst for him for hurting her, but she knew that what comes around goes around and she didn't want that for herself. She pushed out all her evil thoughts and cleared her mind. At least she knew he wasn't the one for her, but where was he? Her one to sweep her off her feet, yeah, it is cliché, but she was an old-fashioned girl. She wanted the cheesy rom com romance, no she deserved it, she deserved to be loved.

She wipes her tears as Nessa smiles at her. "How about a movie night? Horror movies and nachos, we can watch people die gruesomely or suggest better ways?"

Kam shakes her head. "No, you have your hookup tonight, I'll be okay, I just need some sleep. I'm going to close up early and get some groceries."

She looks at her deep in the eyes. "Kam, you know I would drop anything for you even a hookup besides I already heard he's a quick finisher, I can take care of myself better, I'm sure."

They both burst out laughing. "Oh wow...I mean, who told you that?! Who talks about these things?"

They close the store and lock arms as they head to the store.

"I hate to admit this but out of all the eligible bachelors, John may have been the best choice and we see how much of a fuckwit he turned out to be. As much as I love sex, there has to be some substance too, I finally get what you mean. Come on, let's go and get the stuff for some mouth-watering nachos and maybe we'll bake some red velvet cupcakes?" Kam nods as she couldn't stop smiling, she knew just what it takes to cheer her up. She had hit rock bottom today and she could only work her way up from the pits of ex-boyfriend hell.

The room was cold...quiet and cold. Kayden let the tears fall, he wasn't the next Alpha, he was simply a man who is experiencing the worst heartache. There were only a few people in the room and the silence was unbearable, when only hours ago it was filled with the beeps and clicks of monitors and machines, now there was only sobbing. His mother's sobbing...

Heartbroken

Kayden forces his hands through his hair pulling harshly when he reaches the ends. His eyes were sunken and red, they filled to the brim with tears, but he never wanted them to fall. He was in so much disbelief he couldn't console his mother.

"He was just here...and...now he's gone. This can't be real, he can't be..." He mutters and begins to hyperventilate again and is forced to sit down by Evan. Evan crouches down in front of his best friend, his brother, not his leader.

Today, he was simply a child who had just lost his father.

No judgement would be passed if he showed his emotion. "Kayd, look at me, don't bottle it up, no titles, it's just us. Let it out, Kayd, let it out. I miss him, too."

In that moment he could grieve properly. Evan cried as much as Kayden; he was like a father figure who also raised him. They had lost their patriarch to a heart attack, even werewolves could not avoid the toll of having human traits and genetics. Kayden was scared, could this also be his fate, would he too succumb to a heart attack, or a stroke, or maybe cancer?

Kayden please don't think that way. You are not your father. You're so young, my son, all I want for you is to find your love, to have the time that your father and I had, and to watch your family grow. Forgive me, I'm going to go lie down and return tomorrow to start planning the services. I love you my precious son.

His mother squeezes his hand as she's escorted out by her security. She displays a whisper of a smile to her son, the only man left in her life before she leaves the room where her dead husband lay.

Kayden squeezes his hands together roughly, still in disbelief and heartbroken that he'll never introduce his mate or his future pups. He felt like a failure and in that moment, he realized he needed to get out, he needed to run.

Without another word he runs out of the infirmary and into the woods, the wind flowing through his pristine white coat and yet he was still crying. Running full speed, he still could not avoid his emotions.

Once he made it to the falls, he let out a soul crushing howl taking every element of breath that he had causing him to collapse to the ground. He heard his howl returned to him, undoubtedly his pack signaling their grief as well. He whimpers as he hangs his head.

She's near Kayden. I can feel her, she's in pain, she's hurt. Someone hurt her...we need to make them pay!

Phoenix exclaims, growling angrily, but Kayd didn't care about anyone at this particular moment.

Shut up, Phoenix, I just lost my father. I am sure you can give me one day of peace, please!

Phoenix pins his ears back and whimpers.

But...You've been seeking her and I'm telling you she's close but you're giving up.

He sighs.

I'm not giving up; I need to handle my father's business first.

He shut the link between him and his wolf just for a moment's peace. Not today Phoenix, not today.

In fact, he closes off his link to everyone. The sound of the water calms his soul. "Father, I'm so sorry I didn't make you a grandfather nor did I find my mate before you left this world. I feel such a void, like such a failure, what kind of Alpha am I if I can't even find my mate?! I'm the laughingstock of all the packs. I don't deserve this title, maybe I don't even deserve love."

He sighs which correlates to a howl when in his wolf. Defeated, he pads back to the house. He reaches his room without contact from anyone, even the staff.

He pounds his fists against the wall of the shower as the tears and the water cascades off his body. He had no more words, just emotions. He drags himself into his bed and then his door opens, Evan, Brent, and Miles all lay on his bed without a word being said. They were there to show their support, to share his grief, to share his tears. This is why he chose them as his leadership. He closes his eyes feeling the comfort of his brothers.

Coming Together

A week later the services were held in honor of his father, he gathered his strength for his mother during the ceremony. He had moved her into a separate townhouse behind the house by the lake. She had been handling the situation well, she was often seen on the bench facing the pond feeding the ducks and listening to the birds. She would pause for a moment, gazing into nothingness, daydreaming of her late husband and their many precious memories together, not only as Alpha and Luna but as Patrice and Mitchell.

Those memories are what gave her strength when he died. She stayed bed ridden for three days straight. While most stay bed ridden longer unfortunately some never recover at all and he prayed hard for her sanity and well-being. He didn't question why he was fortunate he had not lost both parents; their love was the strongest he knew. Maybe his father asked the Moon Goddess for pity on his mother.

"Kayd, sweetie, are you in here?" He straightens out his tie while looking over as his door opens.

"Yeah, mom, I'm almost ready." She nods as she sits down on his bed.

"Come here, honey."

He kneels in front of his mother and she gently places her hand on his cheek. The tears build up in her eyes and his.

"I never imagined I would be blessed with such a strong, caring, and loving boy. You were our miracle child...I always told you that. I know you've been hard on yourself, but I want you to know that your father was very proud of you and the work you are doing with the pack. He couldn't stop bragging about you to anyone who would listen."

She takes in a deep breath and hands him a piece of paper. "Read this, it's from your father."

He gasps while grasping the delicate paper from her hands. "But when did he write this?"

"Pretty much right after he handed over the pack to you. Go ahead..."

He opens the paper:

"Son, if you are reading this then I have been summoned home by the Moon Goddess.
There are many things I was unable to tell you due to keeping my tough outside exterior as Alpha and leader of this pack. Know that I love you, son, from the moment your mother told me she was pregnant, I was under your spell. You were born to lead this pack, don't let anyone tell you otherwise, you are my son, worthy of all respect given to you. We come off as rude, vicious, and mean but that is to ensure the safety of all those that fall under us. We are protectors and so I expect you to rule with an iron fist but remember son, you have a heart.

You are worthy of love and you will be loved one day but you can't go into it halfheartedly, you must know what you want, and I hope that you get as many, if not more, memories like your mother and I had. Don't dwell on my passing but remember all that I taught you. When you look to the moon, I will be there to guide you. Take care of my Patrice, I love you both. -Dad"

Silence rang throughout the room, eventually sniffles from his mother brought him out of his daze. She had a smile that melted his heart.

"What is it mom? Why do you look happy?"

She brings her hands up to his face. "Because even after all this I still have you and I still have hope." He cradles her hands in his as they walk towards the exit, to the burial fire pit.

Three days later in her shop, "My word Kamari, you did it again! How are you not world-famous and painting for up-and-coming dignitaries of the British Monarch, dining at Michelin restaurants and being swept away by the world's most beautiful men?" Mrs. Preston admires her latest acquisition. "Marvelous, simply marvelous. Your talent is too much for this small do-nothing town. You should live in New York, or Milan, or Tokyo."

Kamari wraps up her framed masterpiece for easy transport to her car. "I love it here, there is no place

I'd rather be. I can't put my finger on it, but I am happy here."

"Really? Even with John and that hussy getting married soon?" It felt like an endless paper cut, it hurt a little and was also enough to affect your mood.

"Okay, everybody knowing your business is the only drawback to this small town. Yes, even after all that drama but I am not going to let that get to me. They can have each other and make each other happy or truly miserable, I don't care."

Mrs. Preston pats her hand. "As you shouldn't! You are young, extremely beautiful, and quite talented and if they don't see how much of a gem you truly are then they can truly stick it where the sun doesn't shine sideways!"

Shocked by her statement, Kam starts laughing and they enjoy it for a few minutes, eventually wiping the tears from her eyes.

"Well thank you for that laugh I needed it." She places a new canvas on her tripod and gathers her supplies.

"You're most welcome dear, now, I will get out of your hair and go show this beauty to its new home. Ta-ta for now!" She waves to Mrs. Preston and turns back to her blank canvas.

She came up with an idea a few days ago to draw her wolf and a mysterious man together, splitting them in half but keeping them together. She started sketching the large head of the wolf, making sure to emphasize the green of its eyes. As she is sketching him, she feels as if he is watching her bring him to life, she feels content. She hits the remote for some mood music. The larger-than-life closeup is slowly coming to life. She ponders the details of the mystery man who will grace the other side of the portrait. She is gathering his stats in her head, height, eye color, facial features, hair color, etc. She wanted similar features to convey they are one in the same, that somehow the animal is his spirit.

Kayden growls in frustration, frightening the people in his office and they scatter quickly. "All I want is a few hours to myself Evan, how hard is that for people to understand? I need to finish this for my mom and I can't because my phone is ringing off the hook and people keep barging in, like YOU are now!"

They have a short stare down before Evan breaks.

"Look, I will hold down the fort for as long as possible, just link me if you need me, brother." He claps Kayden on the shoulder as he smiles before walking out of his office. He locks the door behind him and Kayden goes into his secret room.

Perched on top of a tripod is a near completed portrait of his mother and father, staring at each other lovingly. His hand grasps hers and her eyes are dipped in love. He needed to complete this, his mother would cherish it and hopefully it would take some of the sting and sadness out of her world. His father's birthday was coming up and he scheduled a remembrance ceremony and he would present this to her, if he could get it finished in time. He perches on his stool, leaning close to check every inch of the canvas, adding strokes to bring out the pure emotion in their facial features. He wanted every detail to be perfect. He searches for the dusty rose color for his mother's cashmere sweater and doesn't find it. He frantically looks for the tube.

"Where is it? The sweater isn't even finished and I can't change colors now."

He looks up at the ceiling. "Moon goddess, what did I do to piss you off so much? UGH!" He slams down the brush in the cup undoubtedly spilling the murky water all over the floor. He growls looking down at the mess he created, slams down some paper towels, and stomps out of his supposedly happy space. He's mumbling from the top of the staircase to the door when someone shouts.

"Alpha, where are you going?!" He doesn't even bother to turn around.

"I need air!"

And he slams the door rattling the entire house.

Heading to the garage he chooses his silver Lexus LC 500 and peels out towards the gates which open when security hear the squealing of his tires. They bow their heads as he passes them. He heads to the nearest town: Lovingshire.

Lovingshire

Lovingshire, a small sleepy town with a few amenities of big city life but the residents didn't need all that fancy stuff to be content. They had magnificent views of the mountains that flanked them to the north and the beauty that is Destiny Falls and the river that it emptied out into. There were hiking trails and fantastic skiing at various resorts that pepper the mountains, you can camp in the deep lush greenery of the forests. Not only were there outdoor attractions, but they were also proud of their multiplex theater, shopping center, and amphitheater that could hold concerts, plays, and even the occasional school production. The children loved hearing their screeches echoing off the concave shell adorning the stage. It was beautiful torture.

Kam purchased her shop a few years ago in the shopping center, it was her graduation gift to herself and her leap of faith. She wasn't concerned about being famous or recognized, she just wanted people to appreciate the work that she created, and they did, she had a small list of repeat customers. She didn't make a sale every day, but she had enough buzz to keep her comfortable and happy while doing what she loved.

As she continued her progress on her latest, her favorite song comes on by Beyoncé, Deja Vú. That song always lures her to get up and dance, she was drawn into how sexy and seductive it made her feel, if she only had someone to seduce. She threw caution to the wind and let loose; it was only four minutes long anyway.

Kayden parks his car in the shopping center and wanders around looking for the local art shop; he didn't go into town often, usually sending a pack member instead. He strolls down the sidewalk nodding to those bowing, knowing exactly who he was. He reaches the storefront and notices the beautifully decorated glass in watercolor, the swirls of various blues and greens wrap around as a border as the name is in bold pink lettering: Kam's Kreations. He chuckled at how cute it sounded and that's when his eyes focused on the movement inside.

Inside, one of the employees was dancing to her music blasting. He watched as her hips rolled and her arms seductively mirrored her curves as she danced around, she held a paint brush as a microphone as she lip synced to the song, he focused on the softest most perfect lips he ever saw... the kind that you hold against yours as you pin her against the wall, only giving her the opportunity for air as she moans your name, ravaging her from her ample breasts, running your hands down her hips to her soft....

Kayden: Pull yourself together, Kayden - you don't even know her.

The music was loud enough that he could recognize Beyoncé like everyone else in the modern world.

Once she pretends to hit the high note, she continues to dance as if no one was watching and she looks genuinely happy, which makes him happy. And that's when his eyes focused on the canvas she was working on. A half close up of a white wolf with a distinct ring around his eye side by side with a faint outline of a man, there was only one known wolf like that in the world.

There it was...no, actually...there HE was. There was no denying it. She was still bouncing around but with pencil in hand she calmed her movements to sketch the details of his coat. He pushes the door open slightly, not enough to trigger the bells or for her to notice and that's when it hit him, the tantalizing smell of cocoa butter and vanilla. He was intoxicated by her scent and his heart started pounding in his chest, his hands sweaty, and for a moment his eyes flickered dark and lustful.

As she continued the detailed work on the ears she stood back, admiring her work, "I don't know what it is about you, Phoenix, but you are just so easy to fall in love with. If only there was a human version like you."

Kayd: WHAT?! Did she...no way... I'm hearing things.

Phoenix looks up and rolls his eyes, lying back down.

P: If you would have listened to me at the falls, I could have told you, but you shut me out so you're on your own buddy, peace.

Kayden stands there shocked at his reply.

Kayd: You son of a...

Phoenix interrupts

P: Ahahaha I'm just kidding you think I would miss this moment?! THE moment?! It's her... it's her, it's her, it's her!

He starts singing.

P: Mate, mate, mate, mate, it's our maaaaaate!!! How did she know my name? She said she loved me! ME!!! She's drawing me, there are so many portraits, look!

Kayd takes a deep breath, rolling his eyes hard at this creature who is supposed to be a vicious and fierce fighting machine singing like he's on Broadway, he pushes the door to come in.

"OH MY GOD! How long have you been standing there?!" Kam turns around to meet the most gorgeous green eyes she's ever seen, and they are attached to a nice-looking specimen. Her heart is beating a million miles a minute and it's not because he scared her. What stood in front of her was probably the most gorgeous man on this Earth. Raven hair, swept to the side, olive toned skin, she guesstimated he stood about 6'4" or 6'5", towering her 5' 8" frame, and definitely worked out, his thin white tee aided in her making out at least a six,

41

maybe even an eight pack, and just below that the makings of a big...

"I'm so sorry I scared you, it was not my intention. Sorry, my name is Kayden, Kayd for short." He holds his hand out, his rather large hands.

K: Wait, do guys have gorgeous hands? Is that how you describe them? Cause his are. Why am I moving in slo-mo? Jesus, Kam just shake the man's hand!

She places her hand in his. "Kamari but everyone calls me Kam." He smiles and she feels her entire body buzzing, as if she were met by thousands of tiny electrical currents.

K: What on Earth is he doing to me? Get it together Kam it's just a smile...a beautiful smile, his lips look good enough to...I wonder what else he can do with those...

"Oh, so you're the...owner?" He smiles awaiting her answer.

Kayd: Sweet Moon Goddess, she is absolutely breathtaking and she's mine, she's all mine.

Phoenix growls loudly.

Kayd: Sorry, she's ours.

"Yes, this is my shop, are you looking for anything in particular?" She notices his eyes wandering up and down her frame before he focuses back on her eyes. He couldn't help but to notice she had the warmest brown eyes, but they were encircled by a hazel ring making them unique. Her cheekbones high and her smile, her smile could light the harbor.

He tries to gain composure. "Umm, yeah so I am looking for a tube of dusty rose acrylic paint, I ran out while trying to finish a portrait." She nods and heads to the shelf that holds a wall of various colors and brands. She quickly finds what he is looking for and hands him the tube. Their fingers connect momentarily but it was enough to cause a gasp from her lips and for his eye color to briefly darken in lust.

"Umm, here you go, is there anything else?"

He nods in appreciation. "Thank you, do you mind if I look around, I don't get into town much so I should make sure I don't need anything additional."

She nods and leaves him be while she continues her sketch. Now she was bent over her sketch detailing the bottom of his coat and he couldn't help but stare.

Proposition

*K*ayd: *I have to have her, I need her... her touch, her lips, her body against mine. Looking at her ass now is not helping in any way. I really should have worn sweats, if she sees this it could scare her off.*

P: NO woman would run away from that, hahahaha! Consider yourself blessed, my man.

Kayd: Shut up Phoenix, not during the first five minutes of meeting your mate!

P: Dude, she's hot...it happens. It's a compliment!

He shifts around trying to make his movements less noticeable.

Kam is sketching and noticeably biting her lip. She can't help but take quick glances at this Adonis built man in her store. He looks as if he is uncomfortable and readjusting, she laughs but he doesn't notice but she can feel her own reaction to him.

K: Hot damn what is going on with me, butterflies, hot flashes and I'm tingly all over...wait, am I having a heart attack?! This sounds like a heart attack, maybe I should sit down.

Listening to her thoughts, Kam perches on the stool and leans forward, not noticing how much she is emphasizing her rear. She is determined to focus on her work, bringing out every detail in his pristine coat.

Kayden fills his basket with paint and paint supplies to make sure he won't run out anytime soon, although now he has a reason to come back. He decides to put everything back except for the much-needed dusty rose. He peruses the artwork she has displayed before he stands at the corner of the shop that is littered with photos of Phoenix, or him. She captured everything about him in every situation possible, whether running through the forest or posing majestically. He was in awe of her talents. He could feel her presence before she stood next to him, her scent was enchanting.

"These are magnificent. Absolutely breathtaking..." She blushes while trying to look away, so he doesn't notice. "Thank you, everyone loves these, but I can't seem to part with any of them, he's special to me. Whenever I draw him, I just feel a sense of peace, perhaps even love. I know it sounds crazy..." She trails off. When she looks over, he has a smirk that makes her knees weak.

K: Cool it Kam, remember what happened last time a handsome guy walked into the shop. Yeaaaahhh...

She chuckles slightly as he continues. "No, I think that's a wonderful feeling. You have a true talent, Kamari, never feel ashamed of that. Also blushing looks good on you...it only enhances your natural beauty."

45

She looked shocked briefly, he saw her, making her blush worse and how her name rolled off his lips was simply mouth-watering.

"Look, I know you said you don't sell your paintings, but I would like to make a deal with you, if you're interested."

She turns to him with her hands behind her back. "Color me intrigued, Kayd." She even shocked herself, she wouldn't sell to her loyal customers, but she would consider selling to this stranger? This very, very sexy stranger. It was time for her to live outside her comfort zone.

He turns to her and holds out his hand, she does not hesitate to take it and the tingles immediately cover her leaving her feeling magical. They lock eyes momentarily as he takes her in front of a portrait. Phoenix was resting comfortably looking at the falls with his ears pinned, the moon was full and reflecting off the fallen pool at the base of the falls.

"If you allow me to buy this one, I would like to celebrate by taking you to dinner and maybe you can come to my house to see where I place him, I would be honored to have him grace my wall with such a beautiful woman as the artist." Her eyes widen as she is now facing him and his hypnotizing eyes.

"What do you say, Miss...." He trails off. "Lee. And I would be honored if you purchased one of my wolf paintings. I don't know what it is, but I am content for you to have it." He flashes that smile.

"And dinner? What about tonight at 8pm? I can pick you up from your place." He hands her his phone and she enters all her info.

"As long as you don't plan on kidnapping and murdering me, sure."

K: Oh, smooth line there, Kam. Who says that? Oh yeah, you...see, this is why, THIS.

"Well Ms. Lee, I assure you my intentions are pure. Only to get to know such an amazing and beautiful artist better, if she allows." He places a gentle kiss on her hand. He picks up the large portrait and sets it down by the register and he reaches in his wallet to grab his credit card. When she takes his card, he intentionally grazes her fingertips, shooting sparks from their touch, causing her to smile. Once she rings him up, she wraps up the portrait in butcher paper to avoid damage and hands it over.

"Well Mr..." She plays the same game he pulled earlier. "Miller."

"Mr. Miller, I hope to hear from you about tonight, especially how I should dress." She flashes an innocent smile.

"Ms. Lee I will make sure to send you the details and I am honored you let me buy this, I will cherish this more than you know." He kisses her hand as Vanessa walks in.

"I'll see you tonight, then."

He picks up the frame and the tube of paint and shuffles past Vanessa, who is eyeing him from top to bottom.

It's a Date

"**H**oly shit, Kam who was that walking sex god?!" Nessa dramatically fans herself as she leans against the counter. "I have never seen him before, is he new, where does he stay? More importantly, does he have any brothers, uncles, cousins?"

All Kam could do was laugh. "Settle down, to answer your question, his name is Kayden Miller, he says he stays nearby but I don't think that means in town and I am not sure as we only had a 20-minute conversation after he caught me dancing to Beyoncé. He purchased one of my wolf paintings and he asked me out, now you're all caught up."

Vanessa's eyes widened so much they could pop out of her head.

"Excuse me?! Did you just say you sold one of your wolf paintings to some stranger, albeit a hot stranger, but you won't to anyone else? Are you okay? Are you ill?"

She shrugs off her hand making its way towards her forehead.

"I don't know Nessa, I can't explain it but when he asked, I felt everything in me say it was okay. Like it already belonged to him, so I sold it. Besides, he told me he wanted to show me where he places it at his house..."

She was abruptly cut off. "What?! He invited you to his house, already? Damn girl you must have put on quite the show. So what time is this date?"

Kam looks at her watch that reads 5 pm. "Right on time, closing time! It's at 8 pm..." She starts turning off the lights.

"Well let's go, I only have three hours to make you look like a video vixen." She pulls her best friend out of her shop and they head to her place.

Nessa lived right next door, so she goes to grab a few outfit selections for her because she knows all her clothes are rather plain.

Kayden strolls into the house with his latest purchase and is grinning from ear to ear.

His mother is cooking in the kitchen. "Hey, you're back. What is that? And why are you so happy looking?"

He grabs his mother and spins while hugging her. "My dearest mother, I merely missed you is all."

She scoffs at his obvious lie. "Cut the crap, Kayden James, I raised you." She continues to stir the very fragrant pasta sauce as she waits for the noodles to finish cooking. She was serving a feast due to all the male appetites in the house. Rest assured, there would be no leftovers.

His smile never fades as he sits down, and she studies his face. "I found her, mom. I found my mate."

His mother screams in excitement as she jumps for joy. "Oh, my sweet boy, I am so excited you found her, well, where is she? When do I get to meet her? I have so many questions!"

He takes her hands in his to calm her down. "Mom, you know I want to do this differently than the others. I don't want to rush this, and I want to do it right. I asked her out tonight after buying one of her works of art. Tell me if it looks familiar..."

He begins to rip the butcher paper away from the painting and he holds it at waist level. His mother gasps, she can't believe what she sees.

"How...it's...it's Phoenix, how did she know?"

"She doesn't. I haven't indulged that bit of information yet. She's human, I don't want to scare her off, but I know she's the one, I felt it, the sparks, the tingles, shortness of breath..." He didn't mention the little situation he had as well.

His mother's face is radiant with joy. "So, where are we going to put this beautiful work?"

He knew exactly where it would go, there was no other spot. He would admire it when he was not in pack business. "Definitely my office."

"Did you bring your entire closet?!" Kam sifts through Nessa's selections. "Jeez, Nessa, I'm not giving it up on the first date, some of these dresses are scandalous!"

She notices a deep plum article of clothing and pulls it from the pile. It was velvet and looked to hit just below her knee. "I'm going to try this one." As she ushers herself into her bathroom.

"Whatever, showing a little skin never hurt!"

She checks herself out in the full-length mirror. "Nessa, that is more than a little, besides...I really like this color and fit." She grabs a pair of black peep toes and gold jewelry to round out her outfit. The dress hugs her every curve but not enough to restrict her movement, just enough for the outfit to scream 'look at me'.

She is interrupted by a low whistle from the living room. "You look stunning, girl! Mr. Hot and Sexy won't know what hit him." She turns around to gawk.

"It's Kayden."

Nessa clicks on some sexy music. "That's what I said, anyway, let's sing to relieve some of those nerves you've got." She scrolls her choices and plays a ballad by Christina Aguilera.

"You know how much I LOVE this song." She picks up her remote to sing along.

Caught up in the song entirely, neither one of them noticed Kayden standing in the doorway, watching her move flawlessly around her place. Her emotion flowing through each lyric, she had the voice of an angel.

La Belle Mer

Kam notices Nessa staring behind her but also a wide grin forming across her face. Kam turns around almost screaming in terror.

"Really, Kayden! You almost gave me a heart attack! Don't you knock?!"

She clutches her chest as she gracefully sits on the arm of her couch. He gives her a genuine smirk, presenting her with a bouquet of yellow tulips.

"I apologize for interrupting another...sexy performance. I did knock but neither of you heard me. I see that the lady has a beautiful voice as well."

She takes the flowers from his hand and Nessa immediately takes them from her.

"I'll put these away." She stands and waits for a proper introduction, arching her eyebrow.

"Oh, where are my manners, Kayden Miller, this is Vanessa Vanderbilt, my best friend."

She nods. "Nice to meet you, I'll just put these in water."

He turns his back towards her and roams her entire body. He bit his lip and smiled. "You look absolutely stunning...wow, I am quite the lucky man."

K: Not yet, not by a long shot...not until I have you in my...

OH MY GOD, stop it, you! I'm going to have you committed, I swear...

"Thank you, you look very handsome tonight." She surveyed his outfit. He chose a royal blue suit with a simple crisp white button down and a lavender tie. He looked so effortlessly pulled together.

He clears his throat to catch her attention as she is still staring. "Are you ready to go? We have reservations."

She nods. "Nessa, are you staying here tonight?"

Nessa, not even peeling her eyes away from the television replies, "Judging by all this pent-up sexual tension in the air, I think it's best I sleep in my own space tonight and we share bedroom walls, I'll hear you!" She winks as Kam's jaw drops. She eyes her and gives her the 'I'm going to kill you' look.

"We'll be sure to keep it down then." Her shock now goes to Kayden and his reply. He winks at her and she instantly turns away to calm her blushing.

He pulls her chin back to face him. "I told you, it's very sexy when you blush, don't hide it from me." He kisses her cheek as he pulls her towards the exit.

They pull up to La Belle Mer (The beautiful Sea). Before she can remove her seat belt, he is opening her door as she takes his hand to gracefully exit the car.

He tries not to be obvious, but his jaw drops when she stands up and adjusts her dress.

"Careful, Mr. Miller, a girl might think you only hold sexual intent the way you are eyeing me..."

She looks between her long lashes and he clears his throat, adjusting his demeanor.

"Would that be such a negative thing, Ms. Lee, it only means that I find you beyond attractive and wish to have you underneath me..."

K: Holy crap! WHAT?! Ok, I can't react, got to keep calm...cool down Kam...deep breaths...

Screw that...as a matter of fact you should be screw...

K: Shut up! Shut up! Shut up! Shut up! Shut up!

"But in due time, princess. I like to stay on the gentlemanly side of the road for the time being but don't be fooled, the bad boy emerges when he wants something, I can only keep him at bay for so long. Maybe I'll introduce you one night...if you're good."

Her breathing hitches and he catches that quick jerk of her body. He smiles internally, breaking down her wall slightly.

Suddenly the waitress approaches and smiles widely at Kayden, you could tell she was only interested in him.

"Welcome to La Belle Mer, what can I get you tonight, handsome?"

Kam snorts and rolls her eyes as the waitress doesn't even acknowledge her, she's too busy shoving her cleavage in his face, giggling like a damn schoolgirl. She could feel her possessiveness emerge, he was there with her not this bleached bimbo with way too much makeup on and her dial set to slut. Hearing her react the waitress sneers back in her direction.

Feeling the apparent tension and seeing Kam getting upset Kayden interrupts. "Well, first I would like to speak to the owner about your rude behavior towards my girlfriend, how dare you neglect to greet this beautiful woman and two I'd like you not to wait at our table, send someone with a bit more class. By the way, compared to her you never stood a chance. That's all."

He doesn't even bother giving her a second glance as she huffs and stomps towards the back.

"Kayden, that wasn't necessary, I shouldn't have lowered myself to her level."

He grabbed her hand and his eyes shone in the candlelight and were mesmerizing.

"It was absolutely necessary, I do not tolerate disrespect, not for me or you. I know the owner and we are very close. Now, let's concentrate on this wonderful evening with the most beautiful woman I have ever met."

She smiles. "You literally just met me."

He kisses her hand. "And I've been awestruck ever since."

A middle-aged man soon approaches the table.

"Ah, Alp-- uh, Mr. Miller, how are you this fine evening, I heard you would like to speak with me?"

Kayden's posture stiffens and he pulls his hands from her and she feels the emptiness awaiting to feel his touch again.

"Yes, your server should be taught how to acknowledge both guests when approaching the table, she was very rude. No one should feel neglected as my girlfriend did, and I do not appreciate it. That is all." He places his hand back on hers and smiles. The gentleman nods, turns, and heads to the back of the restaurant.

K: He called me his girlfriend, twice! OMG what do I do?! How did I get so lucky, I'm just a small-town girl trying to figure out her life, but I can get used to this...

"Kam, you still with me?"

She snaps out of her thoughts and right into his eyes. She almost gets lost in lust this time.

"Hmm, yes, I'm with you. I'm sorry..."

A young man approaches the table. "Good evening, my name is Matt and I'll be your server tonight. What can I get you to drink?" He looks at both in acknowledgement.

"I will have a scotch, neat and my lovely date..." He trails off and the waiter turns in her direction.

"Oh, I'll have a black Russian, please." He arches his eyebrows in response to her order.

"The lady takes her drinks as strong as I, color me impressed."

She leans forward, hand gently placed on her cheek, enhancing her breasts in her already snug dress. It takes an army for his eyes not to wander to her delectable cleavage, but he does glance quickly.

"You have quite a lot to learn Mr. Miller."

They enjoy their meal and are waiting on dessert when the details of her past relationship with John emerge.

"It's not something I really like to share; it was drama that I didn't need. All I wanted was someone to care about me and he just...didn't. He was an ass and I wish I never met him. A few days ago, he had the nerve...the absolute nerve to commission me for his engagement painting to that...tramp and I lost it, I absolutely lost it. I rained down on him everything he made me feel and I broke him and to be honest I don't regret it."

She forces a deep sigh out of her lungs. "Okay, enough about him I can feel my anxiety creeping up and I don't want to ruin this beautiful dinner with thoughts of murder."

He chuckles at her admission. "I understand but I am glad you felt comfortable telling me your story. You're right, he didn't deserve you and I will make sure you never think of him again."

Her eyebrows arch in curiosity. "Oh, and how do you plan to do that?"

The waiter interrupts with a slice of double berry, cognac infused cheesecake and a fork. Kayd takes the fork and pierces the dessert and lifts it to her lips. Her beautiful and full lips that slide seductively away from the fork and her eyes close. She lets out the softest moan that no normal person could hear but Phoenix heard every delicious syllable. That's all it took for him to want to jump her right then and there.

P: I want her, right now, Kayden! That was the cue, I know you heard her!

Kayden: SHUT. UP. PHOENIX! I'm taking this slow and at my pace, not yours, you horn dog. Sit!

Phoenix jokingly "sits" but he's still panting as Kayden rolls his eyes.

"So how is it?" He focuses his attention back to her as she comes backs down from her food high.

"It is heavenly, here, try it." She reciprocates and smiles in anticipation as she adds, "Isn't it orgasmic?"

Her cheeky statement causes him to start choking and he reaches for his water.

"Kayden, are you okay?!"

He beats his chest and takes another sip.

"I'm just fine, baby doll, your statement caught me off guard is all. I have a very... vivid imagination..." He flashes his signature smirk, his eyes darken once more, and she feels the heat rise.
She sets down the fork and gazes at him. "Take me home."

Back at her place, "Kam...Kam we need... mmm...baby, we have to stop..."

She had Kayden against her door in an intense make out session. She steps back and pulls her dress down from when his hands roamed her body.

He was trying his damnedest to keep Phoenix at bay.

"But I really don't want to...please...kiss me."

She attacks his lips once again, trailing down his neck and tugging his hair, then she steps back, biting her lip. That simple pull makes him weak in the knees. He grabs her hands, kisses them both, and takes a deep breath.

"As much as I want to and you have NO idea how much so, I want to do this right. You are so beautiful, and I can't wait to make you mine...just not tonight, okay?"

Even though she was upset, she knew he was right. She didn't know what came over her, but she suddenly needed to feel his hands all over and every touch brought that magical tingly feeling she wanted to feel all the time, it was like a drug. If he hadn't stopped her, she was sure he'd be in her bed tonight, Vanessa would have heard an earful.

She pouts but then smiles, placing one last kiss to his. "You're right, I know you're right. Thank you for dinner, I had a wonderful night."

He kisses her forehead, then her nose, her lips, and ends in a gentlemanly kiss to her hand.

"Don't worry Ms. Lee, there will be plenty of opportunities for more moments. Have a good night." She opens her door and he waits for the click and turn of her locks before he turns towards the exit.

P: I. Hate. You....SO much right now. We could have had her, she wanted to.

Kayden: She was impaired by our scent and alcohol; it was lust not love. Don't fret, I will make her mine in due time.

The crisp night air smacks him in the face, awakening his senses as he gazes at her apartment window and he is met by her longing gaze. Even through concrete, glass, and metal he could still smell her arousal.

"For the love of Moon Goddess there won't be a shower cold enough." He blows her a kiss before getting in his car.

Kam gazes at him with such lust and intensity she could not even believe herself, her body wanted him and wanted him bad. She didn't know if it was the atmosphere or the stars aligning but she was out of her element...and she liked it. She was losing control and all sensibilities. She peels out of her dress and climbs into bed but not before getting a text.

You truly are the most beautiful angel I've ever laid eyes on; I hope to steal your heart as you have already stolen mine. -Kayd

She responds quickly before drifting to sleep.

Goodnight, you may not be in my bed, but your name will be all over my lips... -Kam

A Whore named Bridget

Early next morning Kam arrives at her shop and in high spirits, mostly due to a morning text from him.

Good morning beautiful, I will stop by later. By the way, I hope my name left you satisfied last night. -Kayd

She occupies her morning with her fair share of customers including Mrs. Preston who checks on the beginnings of her commissioned work. Satisfied with their discussion she leaves content and Kam gets to work.

Around 11 am her door slams closed and a fiery blonde storms up to her counter. When she calmly looks up, she exchanges glances with Bridget. She doesn't acknowledge her; she waits for her to state her business.

"Are you usually so rude to your customers?"

Strike one.

She eyes her up and down, she can't be serious. Kam stands from her stool, leaning forward, one thing about her height is she could tower over her causing intimidation.

"One, you came in slamming my damn door so I already knew you were only here to cause trouble and two, you are not a customer, I could never paint something so ugly, so loose, and soulless. You want me to draw you in real life, fine, I'll paint you on your knees...it suits you best. It seems to be your favorite position, right? If you're here to ask me to paint your pathetic engagement portrait you can also go to hell with that pitiful excuse of a fiancé of yours. I wouldn't do it if the Lord himself asked me."

Bridget stomps around the counter and sticks her finger in her face.

Strike two.

"Because of whatever argument you and John had, he called off the engagement. Stating that I wasn't right for him and that he hurt too many people, especially you. That he didn't realize just how special you are to him and he was going away to make it right. He's leaving town tonight! Are you so pathetic that you break up what we had?! You act like such an angel when deep down we all know you're a slut!"

Strike damn three.

At that moment Kam loses her control and slaps Bridget and she falls back against the counter. She is in shock when Kam grabs her by her hair to pull her face up towards hers.

"Listen to me, you loose moraled, man-stealing, money hungry, skank... the only slut here is you or did the peroxide melt your brain along with your standards? You slept with all his friends before marking your main target and we all know it was just for his family's money. I'm sure the liquor and cocaine fog your memory so let me refresh it for you. I don't give a fuck about you nor him. He came in here to beg me for forgiveness because you two were getting married, to clear his guilty fucking conscious. But like I said before and let me slow it down for you, so you finally get it... fuck him... and you. I told him how your little 'incident' at the house party broke me..."

Kam doesn't notice Kayden by the door, he was stopping by as he stated in this morning's text. He sees a confrontation with some blonde but it's not too physical and it seems like she has a lot to get off her chest so he watches the situation, besides he can hear everything they say.

"Did you even care that you broke up a relationship? No, because you were too busy choking on his dick like a common whore and what did you do? You smirked like you won and I'll give it to you Bridget, bravo. You got John all to yourself, well, you *did*...I guess that's karma for you. I suggest you take your leave before I put your face through this countertop! I have been beyond patient with you, but I am this close to going to jail with a fucking smile on my face."

She shoves her away, Bridget runs her hands through her hair and wipes the blood from her lip.

"You'll never get John back; I'll make sure of it. I will win him back."

Kam laughs hysterically in her face. "Oh, I could and would never take John back. I don't want anything you gave him and besides..."

She meets Kayden's eyes signaling him to approach and he smiles while walking through the door.

He slides his arm around her waist and kisses her cheek. "...I've moved on. Hey, baby..."

He indulges her in a kiss, further igniting Bridget's anger.

"So, you can get out of my store and live your miserable, sad, and newly single life." Bridget opens her mouth, but no words come out and she screams as she stomps away.

When the door closes, the tears fall, her resolve broken.

"Hey, hey, hey, she doesn't deserve your tears. Look at me..." He lifts her chin.

"I'm just so tired of both of them, I didn't deserve what happened and all she wanted to do was rub it in."

He pulls her into a hug. "Yeah, but who got the last laugh though? You did. Don't worry about them, you have me now."

She stops sniffing and looks into his eyes. "I do?" He leans down and the sparks fly as his lips meet hers. He pushes her against the wall as her hands run through his hair. He leaves her smiling.

"Yes, you have me more than you know. I don't want to see these sad tears ever again. They should only be for happiness."

"**S**o, you guys take it here instead of her

place, huh? No wonder I didn't hear a peep last night." Nessa walks in holding a forgotten bouquet and he takes it from her.

"These are for you, beautiful. I was outside monitoring the situation, so it didn't get out of hand, but you handled yourself very well. I'm proud of you." He gently kisses her forehead.

She takes the white roses and inhales their gentle scent. "Thank you, they are gorgeous."

Nessa interrupts. "Excuse me, what situation? Have you been crying? Was John here again, I swear I'll gut him from neck to navel and gladly feed his balls to the wolves, literally! That bastard..."

Kam shakes her head keeping Nessa's anger at bay.

Vanessa Vanderbilt is one vicious siren if you cross her. Just ask her ex, whose car she painted and keyed the hood. Not spray painted, she dumped buckets of paint all over his vintage Camaro.

"Easy, fire starter, it was Bridget. She came in screaming about John breaking off the engagement and how it was my fault. She called me a slut, girl, next thing I knew I blacked out and slapped the taste out of her and emptied into her just like I did to John, told her how I could care less and..."

She gazes at him, a small smile emerging. "that I've completely moved on. And Kayd was making sure I didn't put her in the hospital, but it did cause a breakdown but not like the one with John that you saw. I'm just sick of being in their drama when I keep to myself and just want what any hopeless romantic wants."

Her shoulders slump a bit and Kayd is concerned.

"Wait, how bad was this breakdown?"

She shakes her head. "Ask Nessa I'm over talking about them; I just want to move on." She steps away to get her supplies for the day.

Kayd eyes Nessa, she gestures for them to go near the entrance. "I can see you care very deeply for her so I will tell you. It was bad, I've never seen her so broken and vulnerable. When she says he broke her, she was not exaggerating, and it hurt me to see her like that. I was the one who picked her up, not him or anyone else, it was me. She deserves to be swept off her feet, she deserves that fairy tale romance she longs for and nothing less."

He holds up his hand. "Nessa, she's my mate...I swear to you I only want to make and keep her happy. I love her."

Her eyes light up as she hears him say that she was his mate. "About time for you, I mean with all due respect, Alpha and I am glad it is with my best friend."

As they wrap up Kam comes back with her supplies and her flowers in a vase. She looks at both of them and rolls her eyes, laughing.

Nessa grabs the door. "Hey sweets, I'll be back later to check on you, okay?" With that, she takes her leave.

He approaches her and pulls her to him, and she sighs, feeling the weight of the world off her shoulders. For a few moments, nobody else exists.

He places a gentle kiss on her forehead. "What are you doing tonight?"

She wraps her arms around him. "Whatever you're planning."

"Well, listen I know it's only been a couple of days since we met but there are some things about me that I need to tell you sooner than later. You've shared so much about you; I need to do the same. I want you to come to my house, besides I need to show you where I placed your painting."

She ponders for a moment. They've only been out on one date and he invites her to his house? Does that even sound safe? He has done nothing to warrant concern yet so...

"I would love to." His face lights up, smiling from ear to ear.

"Thank you. I should tell you that my family lives with me so you may be meeting them. My mom's excited to meet you."

She groans. "You already told your mother about me? Kayd..."

"Why wouldn't I? You, baby, are perfect for me, I don't need time. I knew the moment you turned around after your little dance number."

She sighs. "Please tell me you left that part out?" He nods, giving her slight relief.

"I'll pick you up at 7 pm and I'll make dinner. Enjoy the rest of your day, okay?" He kisses her several times before pulling himself away. His kisses always made her weak, filled with so much passion and intensity.

Kayden: Evan, meet me in my office in 30, I need to discuss with you my mate, she's coming over tonight.

E: Holy shit, Kayd you found her?! I'm so excited to meet her!

Kayden: Yeah, I did but she's....she's human. I'll have to explain to her what I am, what we are, and I'm stressed out. This could get ugly and she may not want anything to do with me. I can't lose her; I have never felt this happy.

Evan sighs heavily through the mind link

E: You won't lose her, if she is your mate eventually, she'll understand, it may be a shock at first, but I'll be right beside you when you tell her.

Meanwhile, at her apartment,

"Nessa there could be a good chance I will meet his mother; I can't look just any old way."

Underneath her long, straightened hair, she seems flustered and nervous.

"You have to calm down, everything will be fine. Everyone loves you, how could they not? You're the town sweetheart." She huffs.

"I am not talking about the town, I am talking about his mother, his mother! What if she doesn't like me? She essentially holds our relationship in her hands, it could be over just like that." She snaps her fingers and takes a generous sip of vodka. Nessa sets down the glass and takes her hands.

"I had the most wonderful talk with Kayd when you went to the back. I always hoped I would say this, he is super crazy about you already and it's sincere, don't ask me how I know but trust me. I want you to throw caution to the wind and live in this moment because after all the hurt and pain you went through you deserve this bit of happiness."

Kayden sits on the sofa near the fireplace in his office and stares at her masterpiece. He felt chills when he looked at how accurate she depicted him, it was as if he was kneeling beside her as she painted. He's jolted back into reality by Evan, Brent, and Miles' entrance. They join him on the sofa and the one across from it.

"And now the big bad Alpha is in love..." The guys chide him, but they are excited, it was his time, he had witnessed so many unions, including all of theirs and every one stung a little more.

Brent pours himself a glass of scotch and offers to pour Kayden one. "No, I have to go pick her up, I'll tell her after dinner." He stands up and looks over his wardrobe choice in the mirror. He kept it casual with black jeans and a fitted white tee. Content with his look, he nods to his brothers and heads out the door.

Meet the Mom

"**W**ell, what do you think?" Kam turns around in a circle slowly to give a full view of her outfit. The skirt of her dress flows around her, it was a 50's style dress that was fitted then flared. She chose a canary yellow, one that complimented her skin tone and wore a white cardigan and white strappy sandals.

"You look like a Stepford wife! Haha!" Kam sighs as she tries to concentrate on her makeup.

"You're seriously no help right now. I'm so nervous I can't even do my eyeliner."

Nessa takes the pencil and completes her makeup for her.

"I tease but you know I am just excited to see you so happy. Now it all makes sense all those talks we had and you describing the love you want. It looks good on you."

She puts down the plum red lipstick she just applied to her lips.

"Ahh, a masterpiece that no man can resist. Take a look."

Walking to the mirror she doesn't even recognize the girl she sees, the simple makeup applied by her best friend only enhanced her natural beauty.

"Oh, Nessa, I look amazing, thank you!" She gives her a bear hug.

"Calm down, hulk. I only brought out your natural beauty."

Just then there was a light knock at the door...

She runs her fingers through her hair as she steps towards the door. She inhales and exhales loudly, looking back at Nessa for support, who holds up two thumbs.

K: Now or never, Kamari. Why am I so nervous?

Oh...it's because you LOOOOOOVE him.

K: I swear I hate you so much. You're a real pain in my ass.

You're not exactly denying it!

She slowly opens the door and can instantly smell his sandalwood cologne, she never smelled anything so sexy in her life. She could feel her heart starting to race as she made her way up to meet his eyes and it was those eyes that pierced her soul.

"Hi." She smiles and leans against the door.

His outfit was simple, but it was in that simplicity that made him super-hot. The snug fit showing off every single muscle, the tight jeans showing off his...

"Hello gorgeous, wow, your hair is different. I like it but I prefer your gorgeous curls. Are you ready?

Oh, hey Nessa, how are you?" She nods to him and they head out.

He holds her hand from her door to the door of his car and what a car it was. It was a Lexus LC, all black, the outside was matte, and the inside was leather.

"Nice, very nice. Now I'm curious about what you do, this is the second car in two days."

On the way to his home the drive is silent as he holds her hand and she takes in all the beautiful scenery along the way.

"Kayden, how old are you? I just realized that I don't know a lot about you besides you sweeping me off my feet."

He glances over kissing her hand. "I am 25, my father passed away not too long ago, actually when I came into the shop, I had just buried him and was working on a portrait, for my mom, of both my mother and my father. My mother lives in a small cottage behind my place and I work from home. Speaking of, we are here."

Her jaw drops once they drive up the private driveway towards this palatial estate.

"Kayden, it's beautiful and it's huge! Are you secretly a billionaire?"

He laughs while opening her door. "Well, not quite..." He smiles and she looks stunned. He grabs her hand. "Come on, let's get inside."

As they enter the home, she is in awe by the size of it and the way the home was decorated in rich mahogany, beautiful glass, and leather.

"Wow...this place is breathtaking."

Before she could get a full tour a sweet, middle-aged woman walks out of the kitchen. She has that beautifully dark raven hair like his and piercing blue eyes. She assumes he got his from his father. She wipes her hands on her apron.

"Kayden, my dear I thought I heard you come in. Oh my, what a stunning young lady. My name is Patrice, I'm his mother."

She gives her a warm hug.

"It's such a pleasure Mrs. Miller, my name is Kamari, but I go by Kam."

Kayd interrupts.

"Mom, did you cook for the group? I am preparing a special dinner for Kam and I."

She nods.

"Yeah, those pack of wolves will be down momentarily to leave no trace of food behind."

Kayd's eyes widened by her choice of words and she picked up on it. She shakes her head.

"Honey, when you have kids, pray for girls, they eat so much less."

With that she leaves, the kitchen staff moves the food into the dining room.

"Why didn't you want to eat with the group, you don't have to make me anything special."

He wraps his arms around her as they make their way into the kitchen.

"I said I would cook and so that's what I plan to do, besides, I'm not willing to share you just yet. So, you sit right there and watch me work."

She was admiring him as he worked his way around this massive kitchen. It was beautiful, chocolate brown marble surrounded the countertops and the deep brown wooden cabinets and even had a small chandelier above the island. He ended up preparing shrimp scampi with broccoli, snap peas, and red bell peppers. He baked some Texas toast to go with it. He went down to the wine cellar to grab a bottle of wine.

When he walks back, he notices she's up and stirring the sauce. He attacks her neck and jaw.

"What are you doing, beautiful?" She squeals and laughs as his hands lay comfortably on her waist.

"I didn't want it to burn, it smells so good, I was being your helper."

He spins her to face him and surprises her with a passionate kiss. It starts to heat up and get slightly carried away. She nudges him, signaling to back away.

"Your family is here, baby. If your mom walked in, I'd be mortified."

He watches her chest rise and fall rapidly, his senses could pick up every heartbeat, goose bump, and shiver but the strongest was her scent and her arousal mixed into one. He was fighting with Phoenix over control.

"You're right, my dear. Let's eat before they come barging in, let's go outside."

He grabs their plates and the wine and shows her the way to the patio. It was strung with fairy lights and had a set of candles on the table for ambient lighting. He sets down their plates then helps her to her seat. He pops the cork and pours both glasses.

"Wow, it is really a beautiful set up, this place is huge, just how many people live here?"

He responds nonchalantly, "I don't know, somewhere between 20-25 people are in the house, I lost count."

After dinner they walk around the backyard and pond area, discussing bits of information about each other. When they head back Kayden hears some commotion in the movie room. They walk in that direction. He clears his throat, and everything stops, and all eyes are on her. There are three large men watching a movie.

"Ahem, Kamari, this is Brent, Miles, and Evan. They are my business partners. Guys, this is Kamari, but she goes by Kam."

She smiles and nods to each one of them.

"Wow, Kayd, she's gorgeous."

Kayd tenses up momentarily and Brent realizes it, looking down.

"You know what I mean. You're a lucky man is all."

Kam notices the tension and moves his face to focus on her.

"Hey, you okay?"

He pulls her closer and kisses the top of her head.

"More than okay. So, I want to have that talk with you if you're up for it and the guys are here to support me and answer any questions you may have."

She nods.

All the men look at each other as they head up to Kayd's office.

He guides her to sit on the leather couch near the fireplace. She notices her painting above the mantel front and center for all to see and smiles.

He leans in from behind the couch, "It's the perfect place, I can gaze at it while I am doing my work at my desk."

She smiles and blushes. "I'm so glad you like it."

He pulls her chin up, gazing at her lips. "No, I love it."

Just as he was closing the distance between them Evan clears his throat, signaling he needed to get this started.

Kayden sits on the table right in front of her and takes her hands. "A lot of what I am going to say is going to be shocking and you may not even believe me, but I swear to you everything you hear from me or them is 100% honest. The reason I need to tell you so soon is because you are and will become an important part of this house."

He takes a deep breath and looks at her for a moment, praying to the Moon Goddess to make her understand.

She rubs her thumb across his hand. "It's okay you can tell me, I trust you."

"Let me ask you something, what do you know about werewolves?"

She immediately laughs and leans back in her seat. "Oh, that's silly folklore to keep hormonal teenagers out of the woods at night and away from make out point. It's nonsense. Why do you ask?"

"Okay, one more thing, why did you choose this particular wolf for all your pictures?"

She couldn't correlate the two questions but decided to answer anyway.

"You mean, Phoenix?"

Evan gasps and turns away, trying to mask his shock.

She continues, "I can't really explain that, I used to dream of him all the time. He was my companion and I just always felt safe with him. He is the closest most cherished thing to me, and he isn't even real." She looks forlorn as they all link each other.

She senses something is up. "What is it? Are y'all going to tell me? I don't like the way everyone is looking at each other."

She sits up and grabs his hands for comfort and he can hear her screaming for the truth in her eyes. He decides to just rip off the band-aid.

"Kam...Phoenix IS real, he's real, werewolves are real, so are vampires and witches but that's beside the point. The folklore you heard all those years sweetheart is all true."

He runs his fingers through his hair and paces in front of the fireplace since she hasn't uttered a word. He's afraid to look at her. Her mouth is open, but no words are coming out.

He takes her hand. "Kam, honey, say something...please."

She blinks a few times as if trying to get her brain to work. "Why are you telling me this?"

Her eyes are welling up with tears and he can't tell if it's from sadness, confusion, or fear. He wipes them away before they fall.

"I promise, you shouldn't fear anything when you're with me, I will always keep you safe." She looks up as he kisses her hand and she does feel comforted.

"Then tell me what the correlation between Phoenix and all this folklore is?" His leg shakes as he tries to form the words to tell her.

"Because Phoenix...is me. Phoenix is my wolf, Kamari, I don't even know how you figured out his name, but you did. The man who stands before you is a werewolf. I lead this pack, so I am the Alpha leader, Evan is my second in command, my Beta, followed by Brent and Miles. Their families live here at the pack house, currently we are on my floor, and they occupy other parts of the house. The moment I saw those paintings it made complete sense. I am the only white wolf with that black patch in the world. When I saw it, I knew you were my one...you were my mate."

Now it is Kam who is pacing the floor, shaking her head slightly.

"Let's just go back a few revelations, just to make sure my hearing was correct, and I haven't completely lost my mind. You're telling me that werewolves are real? Like they roam the woods, forest, and howl at the moon? Aren't they dangerous?"

Miles answers for him, "There are a tiny number called Rogues who do not belong to a pack who mean to do harm, but it is rare they act viciously upon humans, their aggressiveness is always towards the pack that exiled them or did them wrong."

She nods reluctantly. "O...kay, and Phoenix is actually real? How can you be him if you're you?"

K: That sounded so much better in my head.

Ummm...I think you get a pass because your boyfriend just told you that he is a werewolf!

Brent nods. "We can turn or shift into our wolves when we need to, especially when we are threatened or someone we love or in the pack is threatened."

Kayd steps back into her path taking her hands, which are shaking.

"W-would you ever h-hurt me?" He is taken aback by her ask; it knocks the wind out of him for a moment.

"No, baby, I could never hurt you, I would die protecting you. The legend goes that every wolf is blessed by the Moon Goddess with a companion to complete them, to love them and to cherish them. Once we are of age, we spend our lives searching for them, some find them within their pack while others meet by chance or by attending the yearly singles ball, but a slim few never find their mates."

He looked away for a moment, he could feel the lump in his throat at the thought of what he thought was inevitable, he didn't want her to see the hurt he thought he would face.

"I thought I would fall into that group, never finding my one...until you. You are my soulmate Kam; you were meant for me and I was meant for you."

She pulls back, holding her hands up, he physically reacts, feeling as if he ran full speed into a wall, he stumbles back, and Evan catches him. Heartbreak flashes across his face as he looks to him and Evan nods for him to look back at her.
She cautiously walks up to him and places her hands in his slowly, her eyes close momentarily and then she interlaces their fingers.

"Is that why I feel the way I do when you're around, the tingling, the sparks, and the urgent need for constant body contact? The reason why you're always on my mind, in my fantasies and when you're away I feel utterly empty?" She watches as he gently pulls her closer.

"Absolutely, your scent led me to you, it's how we find our mates. Your scent drives me wild, Kam, absolutely wild."

Evan links everyone saying that they should give them space and she wasn't going to run screaming into the night like he thought.

Apparently, there was a bet.

"So, tell me, what is my scent? I hope it's something amazing." He sits down and pulls her into his lap.

He nuzzles into her neck. "Mmm, it is. You smell like cocoa butter and vanilla, I smelled it when I opened the door when you were dancing away. It hit me and my heart started racing and Phoenix was losing his mind. I sometimes think he is meant to drive me crazy."

P: Hey, watch it! Don't you talk bad about me to our mate. Remember she loves me, I'm her inspiration, Jack.

Kayd rolls his eyes and she notices.

"What?"

"Well, when we are not our wolf, we can hear them like a conscious and right now he's mad because I spoke ill of him to you and he thinks that you love him more than you do me because he's been your inspiration."

She laughs. "Well, technically I did know him longer than you so I guess you could say he's right.

P: BOOM! And there you have it ladies and gentlemen, confirmation that I am the greatest! Suck it, Kayd.

Kayden: Oh, shut up, because who's touching her right now.

P: You ass.

His internal dialogue causes him to laugh and her to watch.

" **S**o, can I see him?" She asks hesitantly.

"Can I finally meet Phoenix? I mean you'll still be you right?"

He nods, standing up to take off his shirt and unbuckles his pants before she reacts.

"Whoa, hey! What are you doing?!" She turns away feeling her body temperature rise 400 degrees.

He pauses. "In order for me to shift I have to get undressed, so I don't tear my clothes, unless you want to see me naked upon my return? He looks to see her reaction.

I mean...

K: Don't you dare answer that!!!

"Besides, I like these jeans because they make my butt look great." She giggles and he tells her to turn around because she was practically drooling.

"Don't need you pouncing on my god-like physique...yet."

She peers over her shoulder, rolls her eyes, and scoffs. "Whatever."

"You forget I can smell your arousal and it is oh so tempting to want to take you against the wall right now, baby doll."

She instantly blushes. She hears what sounds like bones cracking and then a small yelp. She feels a push on the back of her knee and a whimper. When she turns around, she comes practically face to face with her inspiration.

Phoenix has his ears pulled back to seem less ferocious but, on all fours, he was still quite large, with his head near the center of her torso. His eyes were now a brighter green which offset his black patch.

She holds her hand down and he places his muzzle in it to lick her palm and whimpers as he gauges her reaction.

"Hey, it's okay, I'm not afraid of you, I'm so excited you actually exist! We were so happy in my dreams together and now it's because I know you were meant for me. This is such an odd conversation...haha but I'm so glad you told me; I have to admit it's a lot to take in but somehow I know it's okay."

Phoenix wags his tail and his ears perk up.

"No matter what Kayd says you're not a pain, you're a part of him."

She kisses the top of his head. "Alright you, I need your human back, please. I promise we'll hang out again, maybe we'll take a trip to the falls." He tips his head in agreement.

She turns around and once again hears the cracking sound, they make her cringe, it sounds painful.

"Okay, you can look."

She turns around just to see his abs before his shirt slides down.

He grins. "Babe, you're such a pervert, your arousal is so mouth-watering right now."

She saunters up to him, wrapping her arms around his neck. "Oh yeah? You plan on doing something about it? I like your earlier suggestion of taking me against this wall..."

She pulls him down for a few teasing kisses all over. A moan escaped his lips when she nibbled his ear. "Babe... we're not done talking. Ugh, I really need to focus and you're not helping."

She turns around and walks towards the couch enhancing the wiggle in her hips, she turns around and sits down, crossing her legs.

"You're teasing the beast and he wants you bad." She only glances up to smile. "So, tell me more..."

He sits next to her; her leg shakes further riling up her dress.

"There are two more things before I believe we can call it a night, for now. Remember when I told you that I am the leader of this pack? Well that basically makes me King and that makes you, my Queen or our Luna. You will have certain roles and responsibilities, but we'll get to that later. We also have to have a ceremony of sorts to officially recognize you. It's our version of a wedding except you would wear silver instead of white."

She nods. "Yikes, two days in and we're already planning our wedding. This has to be a record."

"Actually, it's quite common for us however that comes to part two, for any of that to happen two things must take place. I would have to mark you by biting you, which will hurt! But, only for a second and then it feels orgasmic or so I've heard. It leaves you with the crest of our pack and keeps all the unmated wolves away. We are quite the territorial species and then we have to mate."

Her eyebrows arch and she licks her lips as she suddenly straddles his lap. "Mmm...that sounds like sex. I'm starting to like these rituals."

She teasingly rocks back and forth against him feeling all of him, she stops when she realizes just how ready he was. She is flushed while he looks proud.

"I told you not to poke the beast. You're lucky I am such a gentleman, now let's go to my room." He pulls her from the couch and picks her up off her feet.

"Kayd, what are you doing?! Put me down!" He races down the hall and opens a pair of double doors. He kicks the door closed as she squeals.

He tosses her on his bed and lies on top. "Welcome to OUR bedroom, my Queen." He kisses from her forehead to her chest, his lips caressing the crook between her neck and collarbone, licking it causing her to moan, "Oh, baby, that's my spot..."

His eyes flicker black as Phoenix tries to take over.

Kayden: Not, yet. Another time I promise. Tonight, she sleeps in our arms.

"Kam...sleep here tonight, now that I know you're my mate it'll be very hard for me to be away from you for long periods of time and it will start to affect you, too. Stay with me tonight and then we'll talk tomorrow about moving in together."

He sits up to gaze at her lying on his bed before he gets up to grab some of his clothes for her to sleep in. He finds a smaller shirt that doesn't resemble a tent and a pair of his boxers.

She faces away so he can unzip her. He notices her pink lace bra and the top of her lace boy shorts that lay delicately against her beautiful, flawless skin. She takes over the zipper. "Thank you."

He proceeds to take the coldest shower of his life to combat every sexual tension, thought, and fantasy. He stepped out of the bathroom to see her in his clothing and she looked beautiful.

She smiles shyly before looking down at her feet, he brings her face to meet his. "You're mine." She doesn't say anything but her facial expressions change, there was an air of confidence in her.

"Kayden..." She steps closer and when she is chest to chest she turns around and lengthens her neck. She looks at him as he kisses her lips, then her neck, she wraps her arm behind his neck. "I want you to mark me..."

Secondary Mark

He turns her to face him, her eyes sparkle,

filled with want and need. "Baby doll, are you sure? Tonight has been quite overwhelming, I can wait to mark you. I don't expect you to drop everything to live here with me just yet, we can split our time between places until you're comfortable here."

She nods her head but rubs up against him causing a lustful groan from him.

"I know what I want, and I want this. There's nobody else but you, I'm certain. Please Kaydy..."

He looks at her, brow cocked. "Seriously? Can we keep that pet name to ourselves? I'd never hear the end of it."

She takes her pinky and wraps it around his as they pinky swear. "Sure, baby, whatever you want."

He turns her away going back to work on her neckline, kissing and licking trying to find her sweet spot.

"Mmm, baby, right there."

She moans and her knees go weak.

He makes quick work biting down deep before licking her wound. He was surprised when she didn't scream or wince. She was now looking at him like he was the last man on Earth, and they needed to start repopulating...now.

"You...you didn't cry out?"

She shrugs nonchalantly. "High pain threshold besides it was a split second before the euphoria took over and now...I. want. you."

He continues to back away. "You should feel sleepy now, but your reaction is delayed or nonexistent."

She slides her hands from his chest to his boxers. "Are you telling me that you don't want me right now? Because right now...the things I could do..."

He doesn't realize he's being led to the bed until the back of his knees hit the bed and she pushes him, straddling his lap.

"Kam, how long have you lived in town?" Trying to change the subject into something a bit more PG.

She doesn't stop kissing all over. "Practically my whole life, why?"

He moans as she reaches his boxers. "We should really get some sleep tonight; your body needs to heal."

She looks up and pouts, poking her lips out. They lay side by side and he pulls her close.

"I want our first time to be a night to remember. I want you to know, see, and feel how much I crave you. Deal?"

Her eyes are closed but she nods her head.
"Deal...Kaydy." He shakes his head before she falls
asleep.

A few moments later,

*Kayden: She's not normal Evan, that was no
ordinary reaction to being bitten. She didn't even
flinch and I went deep. She was ready to pounce on
me and rip my clothes off, not fall asleep. There's
something else...she can't just be human, and I need
to find out ASAP!*

*E: She could be part of a pack and not know, you
did say her parents weren't in the picture. Lee is a
very common name; I'll do some research.*

He closes off the link and turns to her. Her eyes
flutter but don't open, he kisses her forehead a smile
forming on her face. He finally had his one and he
would do anything to keep her happy. He snuggles
against her, inhaling her scent which takes him
peacefully to sleep.

Later that night, she was sleeping until she lost
contact with him. She whimpers, reaching back for
him. He wraps his arms around her, kissing her
neck and ear. Her eyes opened to meet his, even in
the dark they were mesmerizing.

"What time is it?" He looks at the clock behind him.

"It's 4 am, baby doll, go back to sleep."

Just before her eyes closed, she felt a sharp burning
sensation near her shoulder. It quickly ran up her
neck and intensified causing her to panic. She runs

to the bathroom and slams the door before he could react.

She looks in the mirror to see a mark forming on her neck, it burns slightly but she can tolerate it. Just then Kayd knocks.

"Baby doll, are you okay?"

She looks in the mirror noticing her eyes are now a glowing violet.

"No!" She's looking down when he comes in.

"What's wrong? Look at me."

When she meets his eye, he is shocked at the color change.

"Your eyes...changed. Blink a few times." She does and her normal color eventually returns.

He looks at his mark on her to discover a small secondary mark that feeds into his.

Kayden: Evan! We have a situation in my room now!

Not two minutes later Evan was in the bathroom with them. He notices the addition to Kayd's mark and gasps. He shakes his head in disbelief, taking relief against the door.

"Oh Kayd...she's...a Legacy, no doubt about it. And when you marked her you woke her inner being, but we don't know what that is just yet."

Kayd looks at her, then Evan, then back to her.

"Wait, I thought all Legacies were dead. We haven't seen one in decades. Not a trace, just fell off the planet."

"Or they went dormant because we are looking at one right now." They turn to her.

"Okay could you stop staring at me and tell me what a Legacy is?! I'm freaking out here!"

Her eyes flash violet again. Evan steps back.

"Whoa, she's a Violet Legacy, the most powerful of the three families. The Moon Goddess must have really big plans for you two. Kam, Legacies are the most powerful beings ever created, usually werewolves but there has been crossbreeding to create hybrids. There are three families depicted by eye color: violet, jade, and amber. If there was a chart for mystical creatures Legacies would be at the top like the Greek god Zeus. There hasn't been much talk about them because one day they all went silent or died, no one knows."

She sits on the counter trying to absorb all the info. "Sooo not only is my future husband a werewolf, but I might be, too? This is way too much..." She sighs and he kisses the top of her head.

"We'll do some research, in the meantime, future husband already, huh? I love the way that sounds." He smiles trying to make her smile to lighten the mood.

Kayden: This is unprecedented, we need all hands for this.

She gasps and jumps back. "You were talking but you didn't move your lips!"

Kayden: Kam, can you hear my thoughts?!?!

"**Y**es! Oh my god, what is happening to me?"

He quickly hugs her, calming her only slightly.

Evan chuckles, "She's definitely part, if not entirely, wolf but she may be something else, the Legacies were known to get around."

She did not care for that last statement. "Watch it." Her violet eyes flashed before they returned to her normal hue.

"Sorry, baby doll, Evan's right, it's just the tales that are passed down, we don't know much about a species we thought was long gone but we will find out. Let's go to bed, it's just about sunrise."

She slides off the counter feeling the weight of a million questions swirling in her head.

"Okay, Evan, thanks and sorry for waking you so early. Tell your wife I'm sorry."

He shrugs. "No need, as our Luna we are at your disposal when you or our Alpha needs us. It is a great honor." He bows his head and heads back to his room.

She sits at the edge of the bed, shaking slightly. "So much about my life has changed in the past 12 hours, I don't even know who or what I am...I went from a nobody to..." She trails off and starts sniffling, gazing at the balcony.

He kneels in front of her between her legs. "Hey, I know it's a lot to deal with, but I am here with you along the way. We'll get answers but right now I need you to get some rest, you might be a great being but even those need beauty sleep." He hugs her and she feels calmer, a smile forming finally.

"Thank you for being here."

He steals a kiss. "Always, baby doll."

Around 9 am Kam stretches loud and wildly, essentially smacking Kayd in the face.

"Ow! What was that for?!"

She recoils her limbs. "Oh, I'm sorry I always stretch like that when I wake up and to be fair, I'm usually alone so no reason to hold back. Forgot that I was lying next to such a handsome man."

She gives him a sexy smile while he lies on his side. The blanket sits low on his hip revealing his V-line and she was impressed. She meets his eye and she knows that he knows.

"Anyway, usually alone? When are you not?" He eyes her suspiciously.

She stands and stretches causing his boxers to rise with her cheeks peeking out and her torso showing, she looks back.

"Who's staring now? Anyway, Nessa sometimes stays over, and we have a sleepover. Oh my god,

Nessa! What do I tell her? Wait, can I tell her?" She starts to panic as she searches for her phone.

She finds it and sends her a morning check in text. It was something they always did if they stayed away from their place.

Hey Nessa Bear, I'm okay I stayed at Kayd's place, I'll be home later, I think. :)

You naughty girl, you better give me ALL the details! LOL see you later, we'll have dinner. Love ya!

She didn't even realize he went into the bathroom while she was texting. He comes out and stands directly in front of her. He leans down but she leans back avoiding him.

"I haven't washed my face or brushed my teeth! Baby, that is gross, I don't care if you were Brad Pitt, I still need my morning ritual."

He hands her a toothbrush.

"Everything you need is there in the closet and I put your towels on the counter, take a long soothing shower because everyone will be downstairs for breakfast. I'll get some clothes from Evan's wife, you two are about the same size." He kisses her forehead before he walks out.

"I'd like to think I look better than Brad Pitt." He mutters as he walks out. She smiles because he does, a million times better, but she doesn't tell him that.

After a long relaxing shower, she steps out in a towel, her hair reverting to her bouncy curls which were wrapped up in another towel. She notices a pile of clothes, a note, and a red rose.

I'm so fortunate to have you as my mate. Come down when you're done, I'll introduce you to everyone. See you soon, beautiful. -Kaydy

She laughs at his nickname, he was right it was awful, but she loved it.

Once she is done getting ready, she opens the bedroom door. Thank goodness it opens right to the stairs because she could certainly get lost in this behemoth. As she approaches the kitchen the noise of conversation gets louder and louder...until she walks in and everything stops.

A group of women were preparing breakfast along with his mother.

"Oh, Kam, you're finally awake! I thought I would have to drag you out of bed. Oh darling, those curls are simply gorgeous, I like them compared to it straightened."

She blushes, "That's what Kayd said." She pulls her to sit at the island.

"And he's right, no need to change who you are to impress us. We are all already captivated, dear! These are the wives of the gentlemen you met last night. This is Camden, Harley, and Jasmine. Jasmine is Evan's wife..."

All the women bow their heads. "It is an honor to finally meet our Luna. We can't wait to acclimate you to living here and hope we can all be best friends." Jasmine comes and hugs her tightly, catching her by surprise.

"Please, call me Kam. I appreciate the warm welcome and Jasmine thank you for the clothes to wear. I didn't plan to stay over but..."

Soon a pair of arms are wrapped around her.

"someone whined like a baby to get me to stay."

All the ladies laugh, and he pouts.

"Hey...that's not what happened!"

She turns in his arms placing a kiss to his lips and the room is swooning.

"Finally, my son has his mate, and this union will only strengthen our pack." Everyone nods while finishing preparing all the food.

"Miss Patrice, can I help?" She smiles at her new daughter-in-law.

"Sure dear, can you make the orange juice? The juicer is in the China cabinet and the oranges are in the fridge."

She kisses him on the nose. "Sorry, duty calls." She hops away before he can pin her against the island.

"Are you ready to meet part of the pack?" She holds his hand and nods.

"Just how many are in your pack?" He shrugs his shoulders.

"Total? About 700, but you won't meet the entire pack until the acceptance ceremony. Just so you know most of the residents of Lovingshire belong to this pack, they now know who you are and will watch out for you when I am not present. You'll know because they will nod or bow."

"Now that will be interesting to find out who is or isn't. Now, what about Nessa? Am I allowed to tell her?" He kisses her on the temple.

"We'll talk about that later, for now your public awaits..."

When they walk into the dining hall everything goes quiet as about 50 or so people, not including the staff, look in her direction.

K: Oh my god, silence is not good. What if they don't like me or think I'm not right for their Alpha, I'd be heartbroken. Breathe Kam, you're overreacting, it's just nerves...

She swallows the lump in her throat trying not to tear up. He senses her nerves and squeezes her hand.

"All, I'd like to introduce to you Kamari Lee, your Luna and my Queen." Everyone stands up and bows.

"Welcome to our Luna, our Queen!"

Everyone says in unison and then applauds. She notices everyone is smiling and she lets her anxiety drain as she smiles at everyone.

Kayd kisses her temple and pulls her chair out before he sits next to her at the head of the table.

She carries on conversations with a few pack members at the table and more once she is on her way out the door, heading home.

"I'll be back soon, I promise." She says to a five-year-old pup named Nikki.

"Luna, will you find me when you come back so we can play with my dollies?"

She was adorable with bright red curls and beautiful blue eyes. She crouches down to her.

"That's a date!" Nikki's eyes light up as her mother picks her up. Her mother smiles and bows to her as they go towards the back of the house.

"You're really great with kids, you know."

She doesn't reply verbally, it's all in the stare.

Hurt

In the car, she lets out a sigh like she had held it the entire time.

"Have we found out anything else?" He shakes his head.

"Evan is working with the pack historian but we're going to need to find others, especially ones who deal with forgotten folklore. We're contacting other packs in search of answers."

She nods and he kisses her hand.

"Hey, remember earlier you asked about Nessa? I don't want to tell her business, but you may want to ask her what she is..."

She whips her head around. "What?! What do you mean? I swear it's like living in a movie, nobody is who they claim to be." She sighs, slightly frustrated.

"Babe, there are creatures who prey on others and sometimes the best thing to do is to hide under a human persona. Just as I came in seemingly human, most creatures do, it's not meant to trick you, it's meant to protect us. She's still your best friend and a great part of your life."

He pulls into a parking spot near her building.

"How did you know? She didn't just tell you."

"She's been a part of our pack since birth, I knew she was going to be very helpful with you coping with who I was but now that we know you're a Legacy she could probably help with that too. Listen, you call me if you need me. I will stay with you tonight after I finish some much-needed pack business, apparently life doesn't stop when you fall in love."

She gasps and her heart starts to race again. He squeezes her hand to get her to look at him. All sense and sensibilities melt away when their eyes meet. She jumps into his lap and she lets the seat back so there's enough space away from the steering wheel. She attacks his face with kisses, she moans into the feeling of his touch, his scent, she just wanted to kiss all her problems away and just be in the moment with him.

"Babe, you know people can see us, I'm trying to uphold my masculine and stern demeanor as the big bad Alpha and it's not going to happen if word carries that Alpha Miller was making out in his car like a horny teenager. I do have a reputation to maintain."

He chuckles but she does not.
She slides back into her seat and huffs, shaking her head.

"Well, I wouldn't want to make you look like anything but..."

She was slightly hurt and irritated. Everything was coming down at once and she just wanted a small reprieve as Kam and Kayd, not Alpha and Luna of the...

K: Wait...I don't even remember the pack name...*sigh* I'll ask later, I'm not in the mood to talk to him right now.

He's your mate...

K: I know that but...it's just too much, aren't I allowed to be a little human and feel hurt?

She slams his door and is up to the main door of her building before he could get to the other side.

"Have a good day, Kayden."

She doesn't let him speak and he doesn't know how to react. As she chokes back the tears enough to see the keyhole, she hears him in her thoughts.

Kayden: Sweetie, I know you can hear me, I didn't mean it like that, you know I would proudly flaunt you any and everywhere. I didn't think that statement through, it was supposed to be a joke and I'm sorry if I hurt your feelings. I'll be back at 7 pm... I love you, baby doll."

His confession of love causes her tears to fall before she could close the door. She slams her door and throws her keys, wanting to scream. It was all so overwhelming, she just wanted everything to be normal but now it could never be that way. Just as she gets her bearings Nessa walks in.

"So, I'm sure you have some questions for me?"

Kam spins around and her best friend is sitting down on the chaise.

"Why didn't you just tell me what you are? It wouldn't have changed the way I felt about you, you're my best friend, I love you."

Nessa pulls the pins from her updo to let her hair fall past her shoulders down her back, suddenly her hair turns snow-white and blows in the wind, but they were inside, there was no breeze. She smiles at her friend's amazement.

"Well, since Alpha Miller has told you about himself, I should too. I am a hybrid, half wolf and half silver moon witch. I have been a proud member of his pack since birth and I had to pretend not to know who he was until he told you everything. We are forbidden to tell humans about our species and that's why I couldn't tell you. It killed me not to but when I saw him with you, I knew you were the new Luna and I couldn't be more excited! You are going to make this pack stronger than ever. The Cheshire pack is the most powerful, most revered pack in this nation! And I'll still be able to hang out with you and visit you at the pack house!"

She squeals but Kam does not reciprocate, in fact, she starts crying once again.

"Hey, hey I know this is a lot to take in, but I'll be right there with you."

She shakes her head. "It's not that, Nessa. We had a blowup when he dropped me off, not really a blow up because I'm the one who was upset and I walked away, it feels like so much at once. Last night, he marked me. I asked him to, I was so certain it was what I wanted, then early in the morning it started to burn and that's when he and Evan noticed a second mark under his. Not only that but my eyes were violet. Evan recognized it immediately. Nessa...Evan says I'm a Legacy. Do you know what that means?"

She reaches over and pulls her collar to look at her mark, there was the Cheshire mark but just below that was a smaller mark feeding into it. She looks at her friend wide-eyed.

"Shit, Kam, you ARE a Legacy! Do you know what that means? For one, you are not human, but you are a special species created by the Moon Goddess herself to rule the world but some time back they all went silent. We thought they were dead! But you've awoken your family line, maybe that means something but I'm not sure what. I'm sure Kayd has everyone looking into it because your union is probably something big, epic even."

Kam groans and puts her face in her hands. "UGHHHHH...it was all so simple back then..."

Nessa hugs her and turns on the television. "I know, so let's watch trash tv to get your mind off of it until he gets back, and you can tell me all the sordid details of last night."

She wiggles her eyebrows causing Kam to laugh. "We didn't mate Nessa, nothing happened besides the bite, the marks, and meeting some of the pack this morning."

She shrugs as she goes to prepare some popcorn. Just then her phone buzzes.

I miss you future Mrs. Miller. Phoenix told me to tell you HI, lol such a pain in my ass. We both miss you dearly. -K

She smiles at her new moniker, could it really all be so simple? She texts her reply:

I'm sorry for my reaction, I know you meant no harm. I know you have a role to maintain but with me you're my Kaydy. It really is a lot to take in, but I can't wait to see you tonight, dinner is at 8 pm... and I am dessert. Tell Phoenix I miss him, too. Yours truly, Mrs. Miller XOXO

She giggles as she hits send.

Kayd looks at her reply and swallows hard.

Kayden: Well damn...

Say Yes to This Dress

"So best friend, what's for dinner?"

Kam ponders for a moment. "Hmm, good question. He made pasta last night so definitely not that. I could do... meatloaf, rosemary garlic potatoes, and roasted asparagus?"

Nessa's eyes roll to the back of her head. "Oh my god, even the words sound heavenly, yes to all of that! So, he cooked for you yesterday? How was it?"

She turns around and leans against the countertop. "It was delicious, who knew someone so powerful and sexy could be such an amazing cook."

They search for the ingredients she'll need. She inventories the fridge while Nessa checks her pantry.

"Hey, I thought there was going to be dessert?" Nessa screams from the pantry and Kam laughs.

"No, I said I WAS dessert. Let's just say I have the perfect outfit in mind for tonight..."

"Ooh, I like this sexy version of you. But seriously, my dearest best friend, I am super happy for you this is the love you deserve. I'm glad you never gave up hope or settled." They hug for some time and wipe their eyes, overcome with emotion.

Once they place the meatloaf, potatoes, and asparagus in the oven, she heads to the bathroom to get ready. She steps out wearing a little black dress, hugging every curvaceous inch of her body, she places her four-inch heels next to the island as she checks on dinner.

"Hot damn, girl! You're trying to kill him, aren't you? Not even the Alpha leader could survive something like this. Hey, this isn't one of mine, when did you get this?"

She smiles over her shoulder. "I'm not a complete prude, woman. I have my fair share of sexy outfits..." She winks as she bends over to check the food in the oven.

"Oh, wow. Kam, do not, I repeat, DO NOT do that when he's here. His wolf will take over in a heartbeat and I can't save you then."

She turns around. "How will I tell the difference?" Nessa steals a stalk of asparagus and pops it in her mouth.

"Easy, his eyes are black when he is in control. I mean essentially, it's still him but wolves are aggressive when it comes to sex, there is no passion or sensual touching. It's still love but we're talking very animalistic."

Kam hears her phone notification from across the room.

On my way, love. Do I need to pick up anything?

Yes, wine and an actual dessert. Nessa's here so you can have me...later ;)

Baaaby, don't do that, I have to go get the wine and would not like for anyone to see my "situation"

Oops, sorry. Think of dead kittens, love you, byeeeee!

Kayd hits the town market looking for a vintage wine he had in abundance in his wine cellar, but because he was staying with her, he knew his choices were limited.

He looks down the wine aisle until he finds it and grabs six bottles, some to keep at her place. He heads to the artisanal bakery and picks up several small cheesecake varieties and a red velvet cake. He goes through self-checkout and is on his way.

Kayd casually knocks on the door and waits nonchalantly. When the door opens, his eyes meet the sexiest, devilish looking angel in a skin-tight little black dress and high heels. She licks her lips before greeting him,

"Hey there, sexy..."

An animalistic growl escapes his lips at the sight of her. "Holy hell...Nessa, get out!"

He is practically drooling as he stands there, eyeing her up and down. Her hand slides down her delicious curves, over the dress she's practically poured into, she bites her lip to finish him off.

"I take it you like what you see?" She gives him a spectacular view of her backside.

He drops the bags at the door and picks her up, tossing her on the couch. She squeals and laughs as he climbs on top of her, placing hot and steamy kisses all over, she can't contain her moans.

"Mmm, Kayd...baby..." He sighs after biting her bottom lip.

"I swear if you dress like this again and she's here, she's going to get such a show. Now...say my name again..."

His eyes twinkle and flash black momentarily.

"Hey, you keep Phoenix in his cage. Now is not the time."

She stands up and wiggles her dress down and pushes her boobs up.

"You're asking for a lot with you looking like that." He utters a swear or two under his breath.

Nessa clears her throat.

"Uhhh...glad you remembered I was still here. I know we've joked about the idea of watching each other with someone but you almost did it and I think I'm traumatized."

He turns his head. "You joked about what now?"

She shakes her head. "No, little miss voyeur there kept inviting me to her one-night stands, she knew I would never have a casual hookup, I was always the relationship type. She knew I could take care of myself."

He cocks his eyebrow and licks his lips.

"Yes, in exactly the way you are thinking, you perv." He shrugs, not denying it one bit.

She plates everything as he puts all but one bottle of wine and dessert in the fridge.

He grabs her waist and whispers in her ear. "Now I get to take care of you every night and I promise you, you won't ever have to worry about being satisfied. I can't wait to hear my name from your lips when you hit your..."

Nessa drops the remote. "Oh my god I heard all that! Hello! Half wolf...by the way...eww."

Kam wraps her arms around his neck. "Don't listen to her." He smirks, tapping his temple.

"Don't listen to my thoughts..." Curiosity gives way and she wanders through his thoughts.

"OH MY GOD, baby, you can't think like that! Wow..." She starts fanning herself. She was blushing hard and her body was quite reactive.

He laughs while sniffing around her. "Mmm, just the reaction I wanted." He smacks her on the ass causing her to step forward awkwardly. She lets out a yelp that sounds more like a moan.

Nessa stands up "That's it, I'm leaving!"

"Come on, we'll behave, stay for dinner, please?" She pleads with her best friend.

"Yeah, but you have to leave after, I was promised a delectable dessert and I'm ready to unwrap it." Kayd smirks and she slaps his chest. "Ow! You're much stronger now than before. Must be the Legacy blood."

She puts another bottle of wine on the table. "How do you know it's not your mark?" She goes to grab the sides when he takes both dishes nudging her to sit down.

"I know that some of my abilities transfer during the marking, but your strength has doubled at least, that is something more powerful than wolf's blood." He chuckles as he digs into his plate.

The Parents

T he next morning, this time fairly cognizant of the warm body next to her, Kam stretches gently to start another day at the shop. She sits up in her bed and glances back, he was snoring, hair a mess, and still looked quite jump-able.

K: There should be a damn law against looking that good early in the morning while I look like I came from the midnight shift at Waffle House in the rain. But I'm not complaining, he's mine.

She turns back so she can push off the bed, but she is suddenly surrounded by tingles and sparks. She squeals as he drags her back under the blankets.

"Baby nooo, I have to open the shop today and I definitely need coffee before I go." She is attacked by kisses and he growls.

"Did you seriously just growl at me?" He kisses her shoulder, up her neck, past his mark causing a moan to slip.

"I'm sorry, what was that?" He smugly replies.

She sighs as she temporarily gives in, turning around to face those green eyes that make her knees weak. She decides to fight fire with fire, she bites her lip while giving her sweetest puppy eyes. His eyes darken and lets out a low lustful growl.

"Let's make a deal, spend the day at the shop and I will stay at your place tonight?" She pecks his nose before kissing his lips gently which quickly gets out of hand. She pulls away, breathing heavily awaiting his response.

"Spending a whole day with you while you complete your portrait of me, with me? How could I possibly say no to that?"

She rolls her eyes. "Vain, much?"

He smirks and retorts, "Obsessive much?"

She gets up and he lets her get ready for work while he brews the coffee. She keeps it casual since there is a 100% chance of getting paint on her clothes, she opts for black leggings and an off the shoulder yellow sweatshirt not quite covering her butt, she pulls her curls up into a messy high ponytail.

After coming back from his car with his overnight bag, Kayd showers and changes into a black button down and black jeans.

She eyes him up and down. "Mmm, nice." She laughs as she tries to get away, but he catches her, squeezing her butt as he lifts her up, so her legs wrap around him.

"I could definitely say the same, but that sweatshirt is too short, I'll make sure to leave some of my shirts over here so you can wear those, they'll cover that nice ass you've got."

She places her arms around his neck pulling him down for a kiss.

"Are you trying to keep me covered?"

"Merely trying to protect what is mine." His eyes flash black.

"Sit Phoenix, I've got work to do today." They share a laugh as they head out of her place.

The familiar aroma of paint wafts through the air as she turns the closed sign to open. He pulls the blinds and lets the warm sun in. He sits at the register as she heads to the back to gather supplies.

"Are you sure you don't need any help?" He wiggles his brows.

"We both know if you enter this closet we won't be coming out. I'm okay, just greet anyone who walks in, please."

He opens the morning newspaper, skimming over headlines to see if any pack activity may have been reported.

As he turns the page, he hears the door chimes. "Good morning, welcome to Kam's Kreations, how may I assist you?"

As he places the paper on the counter he is met with the graceful nod of a middle-aged woman.

"Alpha Miller, what a surprise to see you here! To what do we owe this glorious visit? Here to buy some works of the owner, she is quite the talent and I must say, beautiful and single."

He smiles at Mrs. Preston, "Oh, she's not single..."

121

She raises her eyebrows in confusion. "Oh! Well, it damn sure better not be that jackass John, he didn't deserve her at all!"

He could sense her anger against her ex, and he agreed that bastard would never get her back, she was his and he was smitten.

"Anyway, she is the sweetest soul and I just love her work which is why I am here. Kam! Darling, I'm here for our appointment."

She comes from the back and sets down her supplies on the counter. "Oh, Mrs. Preston, I didn't hear you come in. Are you ready to see the progress? I hope my understudy was polite and courteous on his first day." She jokes as he pulls her to him, placing a kiss on her cheek. She blushes profusely trying to maintain her professionalism. "Sweetheart, not now."

Mrs. Preston squeals with joy. "Oh, Kam you're the Alpha's mate?! Oh, that makes you my Luna! This is wonderful news! Your mate was teasing me about you not being single, watch out you've got yourself quite a handful." She bows her head in respect.

Kam looks at Kayd, "What did you say? Yes, he and I are mates but that doesn't change anything, I'm still your favorite artist."

She nods in acknowledgement. "I'm so excited, I knew that John wasn't right for you and he got what he deserved and you, my dear, got all the blessings owed to you and now you're simply glowing. Love does that, you know?" She sets down her purse and points at Kayden. "And with all due respect, Alpha, if you hurt her, we will hunt you down. We ran the last guy out of town, and you would be no exception, you take care of her heart, she's special." He squeezes her and smiles. "I promise to take care of the most important gift ever given to me." He kisses her forehead and gazes in her eyes, he thought just how beautiful his wife is. He wasn't lucky he was blessed.

After her consultation, Mrs. Preston couldn't wait to go home and tell her husband the news.

Around lunchtime she's working on Phoenix when he comes up behind her. "Hey, what do you feel like for lunch?"

She doesn't respond so he walks around to face her and notices she's not painting or moving, and her eyes are bright violet again.

"Kam...Kam, can you hear me?"

He touches her shoulder and she almost falls off the stool as she is jolted back into reality. She blinks rapidly and her eyes return to their normal color.

"What happened just then?"

She sets her brush down and stands up, the color drained from her face.

"They're coming, Kayd..."

"Who's coming?"

Tears well in her eyes as she tries to form the words she hasn't said in years.

"M-my parents..."

"**B**ut that's good, right? I mean, honey, they're your parents."

She spins around, "No, they are just people who gave me life, nothing more! Have you ever wondered in the short time we've been together why I've never mentioned them? It's because I don't know anything about them! My grandmother raised me until she died, and I was lucky enough to have just turned 18. Never looked for them and I hoped they would never look for me, I want nothing to do with them."

He reaches for her hands to comfort her, but she recoils. "No, I know that if I touch you, it will put me at ease and right now, I just want to feel the decades of anger, pain, and frustration they put me through. Why now, huh? Right when I get my bearings and I'm finally happy. I wish they would go away..."

Her eyes well with tears she can't fight and lets them fall as sadness washes over. She takes her water glass and smashes it to the ground as she screams and walks away in defeat.

As much as he wants to hold her, comfort her, and tell her it's going to be okay, he grants her request to be left alone and searches for a broom to sweep up the glass.

Outside, behind the building, Kam is a wreck as she paces the small patch of sidewalk. So many questions and not one single answer to give.

She takes a few deep breaths as she realizes a good man who cares for her is waiting inside and she just took her anger out on him.

She goes back inside to see he was nowhere to be found. She sighs heavily. "Of course, I wouldn't have stayed either."

Jeez, Kam could you maybe not be such a bitch to those who care about you?

She rubs her hands over her face. She wasn't in the mood to paint so she just watched the foot traffic pass her shop.

Twenty minutes later, her head is down on the counter when the door chimes.

"Go away, I'm closed. Personal reasons..."

She squeaks out the last part as she lifts her head to see a beautiful bouquet of white roses and a 'I love you' teddy bear. He also sets down some cheddar broccoli soup from the cafe down the street, which was her absolute favorite.

"I just wanted you to feel better."

He looks at her to gauge her reaction. She instantly wraps her arms around him, and he kisses her forehead.

"I'm sorry I blew up at you, I didn't mean it. I love you, please don't leave me..." She hugs him even tighter fearing she might lose him if she lets go.

Surprised, he looks down at her. "What would make you think that? I would never leave you, you're mine."

He places his hands on her face, wiping her tear-stained cheeks.

"Don't apologize, obviously I'm still learning about you, I just didn't know how sensitive that subject was. I know that you may not want to talk to them, but they could be a very vital part of figuring out your Legacy line and powers. We need to know that when you and I mate that there won't be any consequences. I'd hate for you to turn into a treasure troll or something afterwards."

She busts out laughing. "What?!" He kisses her several times.

"See, that's the smile I've been missing. Come on, let's eat. I am starving."

They enjoy lunch at the shop, quite an above average amount of people wander in, undoubtedly word had gotten around about the Alpha's Luna. Due to the high traffic, she sells four pieces that day.

She gets a ping from Nessa.

What are you and lover boy doing tonight?

I'm staying at his place tonight, think it's the usual dinner then movies, probably with a few others, you coming?

Nah, I got a do over with Jared, he may be quick on the draw but hopefully that'll just be the first round

OMG, well enjoy...

You say that but when are you and Kayd going to make this official? You need to mate before the full moon or you're in for a world of pain...quite literally...*yikes*

Wait, what?! Why do I need to have sex before the full moon?

I'll let him tell you about heat, but you might want to act fast. The Full Moon is in two weeks.

Okay, I'll talk to you later, enjoy your night!

You too! ;)

She turns to Kayd who suddenly feels her uncomfortable gaze.

"What? What'd I do?"

"Kayden James Miller, did you neglect to tell me something very important about this whole mate process? Something that should be done, oh I don't know, before the next full moon?!"

He sighs. "My mother told you my middle name, I'm going to..."

She cuts him off. "Don't you dare change the subject! What is this I hear about going into heat and being in complete and utter pain?!"

He swallows hard and puts his hands up.

"OHHHHH...Okay, before you get upset, I was planning on making our first night so romantic and special. The deal is you and I have to mate, or you will go into heat, which is where you'll want to do it nonstop the entire time, which lasts about a week."

She smirks, "Mmm, a week of sex doesn't sound too bad."

He groans. "...but those who are marked must mate before a full moon or you will go through the most intense pain, I heard it's like giving birth but twice as bad. It's completing the mating ritual. Any heat after the first one is just a time where you are super horny and want to do it all the time."

"WHAT?! Oh...oh hell no, this is going to happen before then. I will not endure that sort of pain unless I'm birthing a baby. You need to set up our romantic night soon, I'm not kidding! You haven't even seen me when it's my time, it is not a pretty sight, and this is twice as bad as giving birth?! No, I simply refuse and with my Legacy line who knows how that plays into it either! I will not risk my health or sanity."

She paces the floor, rubbing her hands in worry but he stops her.

"Tell you what, we'll go camping and I'll make love to you under the stars. I'd still like to make it a night to remember if you let me."

She kisses him. "Of course, I want you to sweep me off my feet."

He smiles from ear to ear. "Then I'll have it all set up and we'll leave Saturday morning."

She smirks, "I have just the outfit too, if you think the first set was sexy, just...you...wait..."

He looks down causing her to look down.

"Oops, sorry, honey."

He groans as he walks away and she can hear him mumbling, "Dead kittens, dead kittens..." She couldn't help but laugh.

Movie Night

Later that night, at the pack house, Kayd takes her bag up to their room, taking two to three stairs at a time. She was not in a hurry to climb all those stairs and with his speed he was there and back in no time.

She wanders into the kitchen to start popping the popcorn for the group. If she...could just reach...the box! She was by no means short, but the pantry was huge, I mean what do you expect when trying to feed a literal pack of wolves?! She stretched as far as she could even on her tippy toes, she was just shy of her goal.

He walks towards the kitchen until he stops and watches her from around the corner as her smaller frame tries to reach for something at the top of the pantry. Her huffs and puffs melt his heart as she continues to struggle with reaching for something.

He realizes that this is the happiness he's been waiting on, his mother and father's type of love, the little things that she does that cause him to smile uncontrollably, it all made sense.

"Ahem...You know instead of staring at me and swooning, you could be helping me, sweetheart."

He snaps back to reality. "This whole 'you reading my thoughts' thing is disturbing because we haven't even mated yet. This is different from our mind link, adding to the mystery of my beautiful and super sexy wife to be."

She looks over her shoulder as he stands behind her grabbing the microwave popcorn, she so desperately tried to get herself.

"I didn't, I can hear your growling like the creepy stalker that you are. On another note, I'll be your wife when you make it official. I still have human tendencies, Luna ceremony or not, I'd like an actual wedding. I think that's fair, right?"

He hands her the popcorn then proceeds to pick her up and place her on the countertop, her short shorts doing nothing to cover her from the cold surface and she yelps before wrapping her legs around his waist pulling him in.

"Whatever you want, your happiness is priority. Until then will you accept the title of super serious live-in girlfriend?"

She giggles into the kiss. "Of course, I will, boyfriend. Now, before you start something let me off this countertop." His hands slide up and down her upper legs as he tries to control his urges.

She gasps, "Wow! Now I can hear you."

He slides his arms around her waist as he leans into his hug.

"I'm not going to hide my feelings; you're just going to have to hear all of my dirty thoughts about you." She sighs dramatically.

"Don't worry, I have a few times. It's like a to...do list." She licks her lips and smiles slyly, causing his entire body to shiver in response.

Just then Brent strolls in. "Seriously, you two? Get a room!" He chuckles as he opens the fridge to grab drinks and ice cream, undoubtedly for the movie room.

"Get out, Brent!" He growls and Brent holds his hands up in defeat and she places her hands on his face.

"Sweetheart...be nice." He huffs.

"What? I've spent years being tortured, it's my turn now. And if I want to make out with my baby on the kitchen counter then that's what I plan on doing, besides her kisses are oh so addictive." He smiles as he leans into the kiss and she wraps her arms around him.

She just rolls her eyes. "Okay...I get it...just..."

Suddenly her eyes are glowing violet and she goes silent. He waits patiently this time instead of disturbing her. He notices that this form of linking cannot be heard by wolves, it must be only reserved for Legacies.

She blinks several times before coming to. Her face has fallen, all the happiness that was there was now replaced by conflict.

He looks at her, lifting her chin so their eyes meet. "Tell me."

She sighs. "They know everything about you, where you live, the pack, everything. They are coming here to talk to both of us...tomorrow. I tried to tell them I didn't want to, but they said since I awoke the bloodline that there were some things they needed to discuss."

He runs his hands through his hair.

Kayden: All hands-on deck tomorrow, her parents are coming to the house. Let security and border patrol know so that they are not harmed. Maybe we'll get some answers on all this Legacy business.

B: Yes, Alpha, I have let everyone know. Do we know what to expect, what do they look like?

Kayden: Unfortunately, she didn't grow up with them, so I am not sure she even knows. I will tell her to tell them to meet here at 1 pm that way any unknowns are surely to be them. Let's make sure the security cameras are up and running and we are recording this meeting.

He looks back to her and she's crying silently. "I just want to be happy, just you and me, why is my life always so complicated? If it's not one thing it's another." She leans forward resting her head on his chest.

"Don't worry, you got me, and I have you, we can get through this, I promise." He kisses her forehead.

She playfully pushes him and hops down off the counter, pulling the bag from the microwave and dumping it in the bowl while opening a second bag to pop. After the second bag was done, they took the bowls and some water to the movie room where everyone was lounging.

Everyone was coupled up and for once Kayden didn't feel like the odd man out, he was there with her, his love and everyone could see just how much she had made him happy.

"Can I say, Kam," Jasmine breaks the silence. "it is a breath of fresh air to see Kayd so undeniably happy with you. I know the stern and strong Alpha will always be there but to see him smile and be affectionate is nice, too. Cheers to you, our Alpha and our Luna." She raises her water and everyone raises their drinks.

"To our Alpha and our Luna! To the great Cheshire pack!"

They share a kiss before everyone focuses back on the movie.

She snuggles against his neck and he tousles her hair.

He kisses her forehead, "I love you."

She pokes his side, instinctively he jumps. "You better! I hope you feel that way after the visit from my parents. UGH..."

He felt the shift in her mood. He pulls her face to his and kisses her gently, melting her cares away momentarily. "Hey, it'll be just fine. The ending is still the same, you and I building our lives together." She nods and closes her eyes.

Before falling asleep completely, she whispers, "I love you, Kaydy."

He pulls her closer to him.
"You know the point of movie night is staying up together?"

She places several kisses on him.
"But you're just so unbelievably comfortable, and I can't help but close my eyes and dream of you."

He chuckles. "Nice save, baby doll. Night, my love."

The next day, Kam nervously smooths out her floral dress and makes sure everything is in place.

"I don't like this, babe. Contacting me out of nowhere, it's not a social visit, I bet they want something."

He stands behind her and rests his hands on her shoulders.

"We don't know anything, maybe they want to see their baby girl after all these years."

She shakes her head and walks to the window facing the front of the house. "Yeah, right. Next you'll tell me our President is a werewolf."

He goes deathly silent and her eyes widen. "No way?!"

He busts out laughing. "I'm kidding, but you never know, maybe one day."

She smacks his chest. "That is not funny!"

B: *Alpha, her parents are in the living room.*

They didn't walk up to the door, they seemed to have just...appeared, like out of nowhere.

Kayden: O....kay. Let them know we'll be down momentarily.

He snaps out of the link, trying to find the best way to tell her. He decides to just rip off the band aid.

"Baby doll, they're downstairs."

She looked confused. "How? I didn't see them pull up or even walk to the door?" He shrugs and reaches for her hand.

With one last sigh, she takes his hand as they leave the bedroom.

When Kam's heels hit the last stair, she looks up and sees two figures seated on the couch. Evan nods, linking Kayd some info, before standing guard by the main exit.

"Do you want to go alone? I know this is a sensitive subject, I can wait right here, whatever you want me to do."

She adamantly shakes her head. "No, baby please come, I need you with me." He kisses her temple as her parents hear their whispering and they stand and turn around to face their daughter.

She takes notice of her mother first, she was the spitting image of her but younger and rocking her natural curls, her mother's pressed straight into an elegant updo. She held a regal posture that further emphasized her beauty and highlighted a feature she knew too well; her piercing hazel eyes. Even though she only had just the distinct ring around her brown eyes she was now looking at the source.

Her mother's eyes now filled with tears as she tries to speak but she can't. She whispers her daughter's name, but no sounds come out.

Her father takes his wife's hand and pats it gently. He stood tall and powerful, was the best way to describe him, she noted some similar features they shared including his warm brown eyes and flawlessly beautiful cocoa skin color. He merely nodded in her direction, waiting to see her first reaction to them standing before her.

Kamari stands before her parents and it is completely silent. Kayd notices the intensity and whispers in her ear.

"Ahem, mother, father it's nice to finally meet you after...ALL this time..." Her words are sharp but sincere. She was happy to see them but there was much to explain.

Her father steps forward, "We have waited so long to see you, Princess Kamari. We have missed you and we know that we owe you an explanation." Her mother nods in agreement.

"P-princess?" She stutters as Kayd gestures that everyone sits down as he feels her knees weakening, seconds from collapsing.

Her mother wipes her tears and smiles. "Yes, sweetheart, you are our last and only heir to the Violet Legacy bloodline. We had to wait for you to find your mate and for you to be marked before we could come out of hiding and find you. We are forbidden any contact until then but I... missed you so..."

"But why are you hiding? Am I in danger? Are you?" Her questions a mile a minute and they just shake their heads, calming her fears.

Her father eyes her mate. "My apologies Alpha Miller, we have not been properly introduced, I am King Malcolm Remington of the Violet Legacies and this is my wife, Queen Melody Lee-Remington." The men shake hands and Kayden bows to her mother.

"It is a great honor to meet you, thank you for coming here to finally get some answers for her. As family I want you to know of the special events coming, I know she would love having you there. We are planning the Luna acceptance ceremony as well as a proper human wedding. My only responsibility is her happiness, just know I will come in between anyone and anything that hinders that, I don't care who they are..."

She notices his eyes flash black, Phoenix wants control, but they revert to the beautiful green she swoons over. "Keep control of him, please." He nods, shifting in his seat.

"That seems reasonable, Alpha Miller. I am honored that such a powerful man has been deemed fit for our princess..."

Kam holds up her hand, "Yeah about that... let's go back to my title, am I truly a Princess?" They both nod their heads.

"The moment he marked you, your royal blood was coursing through your veins. When an heir is marked is when he or she is gifted their Legacy powers and official title. Each Legacy offspring is mated to a very powerful being which is usually a werewolf or vampire. The bond causes their offspring to be twice as powerful as their parents. You, my sweet daughter, are a Legacy with the powers of my werewolf and your mother's white witch. However, I must warn you that when seriously threatened you can conjure up dark magic as well to protect those under you. Legend has it that the offspring of the three Legacy families will be hidden away until they find their mates. That's why you have your mother's maiden name so no one could find you, the power possessed once their mate was found would be tremendous and the combination with an Alpha leader would make them the most powerful pack..."

She sits there in awe of all the information. "But beware, you are the first of the Legacy children to find their mate but not the last and you could be challenged for power. Right now, the Amber and

Jade children are in their teenage years but who's to say they won't be power hungry once their mate is found and come after you. A power shift could change among the families and currently we hold the power. If you bear a child before either finds their mate, that child's power will be twice the strength you now have, which is already quite powerful, I can sense it on you, my dear. That child will precede all other Legacies and will automatically be the most powerful being ever and so will their pack."

She looks at Kayd then her parents, she shakes her head. "Tell me, how could you abandon me like that? Was I not enough? Didn't you love me? All this information is great, but it doesn't give me the one answer I need...why did you leave me?"

Her eyes fill with tears so quickly that he could only wipe them away with his thumb while he hands her a Kleenex.

He wraps his arm around her and squeezes her hand with the other. She shakes her head, the pain taking over.

"Hey, look at me. Give them a chance to explain. I'm right here if you need me, baby." He kisses her forehead. She nods as she places her forehead against his. "Thank you."

"Kamari, sweetheart, we were forced to give you to a family member who was posing as a normal human being so you could have a regular life and not have to deal with the powers you were going to inherit, unfortunately it is decreed, and we can't go against our supreme elders. Of course, we love you, every single second of every single day! Your grandmother restricted our contact, she knew we could derail your progress and though it pained us tremendously you turned out so well. We are so proud of you and we can only hope that you can begin to forgive us. We know it will not be overnight, we only want to spend time with our baby girl." She merely nods, too many emotions to express.

Kayd clears his throat, "Well, I have some questions about her powers. She can already read my thoughts, is that normal? If she is part wolf, where is her wolf?"

Her dad turns to her. "Kamari, sweetie, do you find yourself talking to your conscience? Does it feel like a conversation with another voice that isn't yours? That is probably your wolf talking, you should introduce yourself. Every Legacy is different, we don't know if you'll get full power of your wolf or even your witch, you'll have to be monitored and trained."

Kayd looks at her and she shakes her head. "And here I thought I was just talking to myself." He smiles.

"Has she told you her name? Phoenix is dying to know." She shakes her head.

K: I guess it does make sense now that you were always trying to give me advice, keep me on the right path.

Unknown: You're damn right I did! If I told you who I was you'd admit yourself to the nearest psychiatric ward. I had to hide myself away deep within but now you're powerful enough to deal. I am your wolf, Tatiana. It is a pleasure to formally meet you Princess Kamari.

K: Just call me Kam and I am so happy you are with me.

T: Yeah, so is Phoenix, I've never seen a wolf act like such a love-sick puppy. Is he always like this?

Kayd laughs out loud, her parents look at him confused.

"I'm sorry, my wolf just met hers and he's over the moon. So, the next question is kind of personal, but will we have any problems when we mate and have puppies?"

A look of shock crosses their faces as they look at each other before looking back at them.

"You...haven't mated yet?"

"Oh, my god..." Kam puts her face in her hands, embarrassed couldn't even compare to how she was feeling right now. He answers due to her mortification. They were still her parents and here they were having the sex talk.

"I have something planned for us, I never wanted to rush her into anything no matter what. I have been around long enough to see how others react to finding their mates and I simply don't want that, I want to romance her and love her, not just mark and mate her. I'm curious, the way you contacted her... by the link, is that use only for Legacies?"

Her dad shakes his head, "The power of the Legacies goes both ways. When you complete the...process, you will also be able to link with us and other Legacies and you will become stronger than you already are."

Kayd shifts in his seat. "Another touchy subject, I marked her but if we don't mate initially before the full moon she will go into heat, do you go through something like that?"

"Oh! Umm, unfortunately we do. The pain actually doubles with Legacies so for her it would be...four times as bad...I'm sorry, Kammi Bear." Her mother flinches, having to break the news.

Kam shoots straight up. "Are you freaking kidding me?! What...the...bloody hell?! I'm not seeing any positive point to this Legacy stuff! Four times as bad as giving birth, like real birth?! Yeah, we're not going to give that a chance. I'm sorry for being so crass, mother... father. Kayden James, I swear, if you don't plan something, neither of us are going to survive the full moon..."

She's practically in tears as he kisses her hand. "I already have," He kisses her temple "it's going to be magical, just needed to know you'd be okay." His gaze melts her from the inside out and she couldn't help but smile, which was his weakness.

She taps her temple, making sure only he sees her signal.

K: If they weren't here, we'd be fixing this situation now! I'm so serious Kayd, I can't go through that if I'm not actually pregnant. I seriously feel a panic attack coming on...

146

Kayden: I know, sweetheart, please don't. I assure you I have quite the romantic weekend planned; I swear to you. I want you to see and feel how much I cherish you and need you. I'm going to make love to you all weekend...perhaps we'll start our family early.

K: Ha! Absolutely not, I am and will stay on the pill. Besides, we haven't had our ceremonies yet. Call me a traditionalist but you still owe me a proposal, a ring, and a wedding date.

She smiles and they share a laugh as their parents just watch their interaction. They smiled at each other while holding hands, their daughter was happy and in love and that's all that mattered.

"Mom, dad you know I have a million more questions, but I don't want to overwhelm you today. As much as I didn't want you to, I am so glad you came. Give me a few days before we go any further is all I ask. Will you stay in town, maybe stay at my place?"

Kayd shakes his head. "No, I own the new Harbor Estate homes in town. You will stay in one of the furnished residences." They nod.

Her dad takes her hand and pulls her into a hug. "My beautiful and amazing daughter I am so sorry we had to put you through so much, but your reign will be great and powerful. Now that our hibernation is over, we will be available to you no matter where we are. We love you dearly, Princess."

147

When he kisses her forehead, it releases decades of pent-up emotions and frustrations. It was that kiss that allowed her to shed it all. Her mother joins in the family embrace. Although he would never admit it, Kayd shed a few tears watching them embrace, as well. He felt relief and he sensed her relax, finally. She was somewhat at peace.

K: Tati if I could, I'd hug you too. I'm thankful for your help and your friendship, even when I yelled at you.

T: Thank you, Princess. I am here to protect you and Alpha in any way. I like seeing you so happy, it beats when you were with John. What a waste of a werewolf...

K: What?! He was a...

T: Oh yeah, he was a... pathetic excuse for a werewolf or a man. Do you remember suddenly getting the urge to search for him at the party and then...you know, the big reveal? That was me pushing you to see the truth so we could move the hell on from his sorry ass. I'm sorry he hurt you, but I couldn't let you go further. I mean, you contemplated marrying him, he was and IS beneath you, he was never good enough.

K: I... you're right...

By the time she realizes she's been quiet the entire time, all eyes are on her. Her mouth was wide open and Kayd was concerned.

"Baby doll, what is it?"

She shakes her head, but he rebuts "You know you can tell me anything." She takes a deep breath, still shocked by Tati's revelation.

"Tati told me that she was the one that coaxed me to find John in that precarious situation to rid myself of him because I actually thought... I thought I wanted to marry him."

She meets his eyes and his jaw clenched so tightly at the last statement.

"Please don't do that..." She places her hand on his cheek and his jaw trying to let her touch ease his anger.

"I was so blind, how could I ever think he was anywhere near husband material, he was weak and dishonest, he literally lied to my face even after the last confrontation he couldn't even admit to what he did or that it was wrong, he just passed along a sorry ass apology and expected me to accept. But you, my love, have shown nothing but compassion and patience while trying to figure out this Legacy ordeal. You have shown me the meaning of real love and I am so thankful for you." All tension releases as he pulls her close, sharing a few kisses and a big smile. "I love you." He states briefly.

Concerned, her mother looks at them, "Where is this John fellow now?"

She shrugs her shoulders. "Apparently, after our last confrontation at my art studio, John Michael Evans has left town with his tail between his legs."

The men exchange glances and Kayd's links Evan, he blocks the link between he and Kam.

Kayden: Evan put John Michael Evans on our rogue watch list and tighten security around the compound and for Kam and her parents. I want to know where he ran off to and who he's been talking to. I don't trust that he just left after confronting Kam.

E: Who is he? His name sounds familiar.

Kayden: He was the lying bastard who cheated on Kam at the house party then asked her to paint his engagement photo with the girl he cheated on her with. While we are at it, add her to the list, Bridget McClain.

E: Bridget?! He was going to marry Bridget, the town...never mind. He definitely did not upgrade, he plummeted.

Kayden: One man's loss, my man...

E: They are both on the watch list, sir. All set.

He focuses back as he notices that she is squeezing his hip bone to bring him out of link.

"Sorry, my Princess, giving Evan some commands and beefing up security. I agree with your parents about being uncomfortable not knowing his whereabouts or intentions. Something isn't right."

To the Falls

T hey bid her parents farewell as they are taken,

by private car, to their temporary residence. She
never did get to ask how they just appeared on pack
grounds, perhaps next time.

She takes Kayd's hand and turns towards the front
doors. "Thank you, you didn't have to allow them
on pack ground or into your home, but you did and
I'm grateful for it."

He quickly shakes his head. "They are your family
and they are always welcome on pack ground and in
OUR home." She looks shocked. "Listen, I know it
sounds like a lot, but we don't have to live in the
main house, we can pick one of the cottages or town
homes. We can even live in town though it would
be quite difficult to keep up a low profile."

He wraps his arms around her, and she is floating in
his warmth. "Kayd...I... I can't leave my shop, it's
my baby. I worked hard for that."

He turns to face her. "I understand, I would never
ask you to give it up. Let's hire someone from the
pack to take over and manage it. I have everyone's
resumes; we can go through them and pick
accordingly. You can paint in my art space, but
Kam, we need to start your training, both Luna and
combat. I'd die if you got hurt or were in any danger
without being able to take care of yourself if I'm not

there. We have the best trainers and the ladies can help you go over your future Luna duties. Let's not forget that mysterious Legacy aspect, we have to find out your powers and learn how to maintain them, maybe even strengthen them."

She looks down at her form, "Well I do need to hit the gym, I've neglected it since Jo--it's been a while. Actually, let's go for a run. No better time than the present. How far is it to the falls?"

He ponders for a minute. "I think it's about two miles, I never thought about it because I'm always in my wolf and we run at full speed, it takes me no time to get there."

She rolls her eyes. "Well, we're all not that lucky, sweetheart." He picks her up and runs up the stairs to their room. "If you keep doing that I'll never get in shape!"

She walks into the closet, it was fully furnished on both his and her sides, he had them buy her a whole new wardrobe. She searches the drawers for athletic wear choosing black crop leggings and a pink sports bra. She pulls her hair up into a poof and walks out.

"Okay, I'm ready."

Suddenly she hears growling, turns around to see a half-naked Kayd, rather Phoenix, staring at her, his eyes black as night. She steps back as he steps forward.

"Phoenix, baby, calm down...let's take a run to the falls, okay? I owe you some 'me' time anyway, please?"

He tilts his head like a puppy then bows his head as he shifts into full wolf. He playfully pounces on top of her and starts licking her face before he moves down to his mark, eliciting a moan. He knew he did it on purpose and so did she. She bites her lip causing him to whimper, playing on his weakness. She grabs her music and walks out their door.

Outside, she puts her ear buds in and searches for her playlist. She nods to him

"Give me a five-minute head start, okay, sweetie?" She places a kiss between his eyes as she sets off.

The view was beautiful as she passed by the lush greenery of the forest with sunshine peeking through the crevices, the red poppies that grew on the forest floor, the land was beautiful and seemingly untouched.

Kam could feel her chest tightening reaching her labored running phase, but she kept moving, her music keeping her on pace. The other motivation is that her boyfriend, or his wolf, would be catching up to her at any moment now.

Twenty-five minutes later, she comes up on the falls, removing her earbuds to listen to the beautiful sound of water crashing. She climbs over the wooden fence and is awestruck by the spectacular view.

A few moments later she heard the pad of Phoenix's feet as he sits next to her and she leans against him.

"I regret that, I regret ALL of that. I know you let me win but I'll take it. You know Phoenix, I know your 'boss' can hear me as well, but you have been a really great inspiration to me. You got me through some of the toughest moments of my life because I could focus on painting you and when I was with you, I was happy. You're amazing when you're not trying to hump me, but I get that too. We'll be connected very soon and then I can live my life happily ever after with both of you."

She smiles as he brushes his head against her shoulder and licks her face. She can't help but giggle as he tries to knock her over again.

"Alright, we'll do this again but it's getting chilly and I need your 'boss' back for his body heat. I love you, Phoenix, don't ever change." As he shifts back, she goes into her bag to retrieve his sweats and t-shirt. She is staring, mouth wide open as she gazes upon his naked frame, his sweaty... muscular ...blessed, naked body.

"Oh, sweet mother of God..."

She tosses his clothes as she turns around suddenly, blushing and about 100 degrees warmer.

He slips his arms around her shoulder, pulling her against him and he kisses her temple.

"Mmm...I can smell it all over you, baby doll, your arousal is intoxicating. Just wait until Saturday."

They lock eyes before walking towards the house. "Phoenix told me to tell you that he loves you and Tati more now than ever. Can't say that I blame him, that's how I feel, too." He kisses her forehead.

"He's such a sweetheart."

He turns her around. "Hey, I'm really starting to think you do love him more than me." He pouts but she brings her lips to his.

"Don't tell me you're jealous? Aww, you know I love you both equally, I've just known him longer and I'm still getting to know you, even though we have two ceremonies planned. Like, remember you told me you were painting a portrait for your mom when I first met you, how often do you paint and where do you do it?"

She starts pulling him toward the house before he could answer and that's when familiarity hits.

At that moment Kayd's eyes widen, looking down as her hand pulls him. His face is pure shock as if he just discovered something.

"Sweet Moon Goddess...it was you! Every time I painted a portrait, I always wondered who she was...but she was...YOU."

She looks at him blankly until he picks her up piggy-back style and runs back to the house. He links his command to meet them in his office.

In no time they are back at the house and he sets her down but drags her through the house and up to his office.

"Alpha, Luna, what was so important?" Kayden starts laughing. Everyone looks at him like he's a madman, but he continues as he sits down in his chair and places her on his lap.

His laughter subsided, "I'm sorry I just had a revelation, everyone knows I love to paint and that I do paint somewhere in the house but only my command and a few others know exactly where my sanctuary is."

Evan nods as Kayd pats her bottom to signal her to stand up. "Kam, sweetheart, it all makes sense now." He pulls her to the bookcase and Miles, Evan, and Brent stand up. He points to a book of The Odyssey, his favorite. "Pull that one." He tells her and she does so causing the wall to slide back. He pulls her through and when she walks in, she realizes just what he meant.

Not only had she been drawing him, but he had drawn her, pulling his hand towards the most beautiful sites around town. Her face was never visible, but she could tell it was her, the hair was a dead giveaway.

She gasps, "How...how long have you been drawing... me?" She does a slow turn along with everyone else until he takes her hands.

"For the longest time, one day this gorgeous girl came to me in a dream and she was pulling me towards the falls, but I could never see her face, but I knew she was my one. I was just so happy when we were together, I wanted to find her, I needed to find her...and I did, I found you." She smiles and presses her lips to his.

The guys cough loudly to catch the lovebird's attention. Evan claps his back and smiles. "It all makes sense. It's a spitting image of her, no one will believe this unless they see it. You need to hang them together." She peruses all the paintings until she stops at the one that takes her breath away. It was a winter backdrop of her pulling him towards the falls. "Definitely that one, it emphasizes the white of your coat in my painting."

The guys work to place the photo on the adjacent wall next to hers. He had a perfect view of both portraits.

As everyone exits the office he turns to his command.

"Remember, you're in charge this weekend as your priority is to keep the pack safe while we are gone." They all nod and bow to them.

He turns to her, "And you should start packing for our camping trip tomorrow." He smacks her butt as she yelps and runs towards their room with him close behind.

Cabin in the Woods

The alarm goes off at 6 am and they both groan simultaneously.

"Ugh, whose great idea was it to get up this early?"

She smacks his chest not needing an answer, she was already blaming him.

She sits up and stretches gingerly, squeaking just out of his grasp as he tries to coax her back to bed.

"No, no, no, you said we need to be on the road by 8 am. Come on, sweet cheeks, just think of all the FUN we'll have." She hears him growl from their walk-in closet and before she knew it his hands were wrapping around her, attacking her all over until she convinced him to get ready.

After getting dressed, a light breakfast, and saying goodbye to his mother, who was up prepping breakfast for the pack members at the house, they both hop into his Jeep Grand Cherokee and wave goodbye to those who were awake at this ungodly hour.

He places his non-driving hand on her knee, catching her attention.

"Hey, baby doll, it's a three-hour drive, why don't you get some rest until then."

She looks at him, concerned. "Are you sure you'll be okay by yourself?" He simply nods, tuning to his favorite radio station as she reclines her seat and closes her eyes.

During that time Kayd glances over occasionally to watch his Sleeping Beauty. His mind wandered because for someone so innocent she wielded a great deal of power without even realizing.

Her Legacy powers, that were once dormant, were starting to emerge. He realized her eyes turned violet when she displayed deep emotion or reaction, but the newest revelation is her ability to create a force field while learning about protection spells from her mother. When she was in power as her white witch her once curly locks would fall straight down her back and turn a deep purple in color, much like her eyes, signaling her readiness to defend those she cared about. Though no need to use her newfound powers it was good she got them in her control.

She would be a warrior for her pack, but she would also be a secret weapon if need be.

The only mystery now was the impact their mating would have on her powers and essentially his.

Kam is awakened when she feels him running his hand up and down her thigh causing her to breathe heavily, almost panting. She opens her eyes slowly to watch his hand move up and down until he glances over.

"We're almost there, I didn't want to startle you."

She yawns and stretches. "So, you decide to work me up instead?" She looks out the window at their surroundings. The view was picturesque as they were surrounded by thickets of lush green forest but there was a clearing in the trees that led to a beautiful crystal-clear lake. Around the perimeter of the lake were six igloo style cabins where the top half of the bedroom ceiling was clear to enjoy the stars at night. The spacing between the igloos supplied enough privacy from the next.

He opens her door then retrieves their bags. She adjusts her khaki shorts, ties her tank top into a knotted crop top and ties her plaid shirt around her waist, giving him quite the view. She did it on purpose to rile him up for his actions earlier, all he could do was growl and roll his eyes. She loved being a tease.

He goes to the reception cabin while she stands near the lake. She takes in the sharp, crisp, clean air and the beauty of the surroundings overall, it was absolutely breathtaking. When he had suggested camping, she took it in the traditional sense with tents and sleeping bags, but this was different, she always had this on her bucket list.

"Hey, baby doll, I got our keys, we have cabin number six. Here, open the door and I'll get the rest of our stuff."

She runs up to him, planting a quick kiss before taking the key and basically skipping to the cabin. The size of the cabins was greatly different from where you park to standing in front of one. They were massive, much like a normal cabin but with an added skylight bonus. As he approaches, she opens the cabin and is in awe. The door opened into the open layout of the living area and kitchen in the rear.

She noticed a vase of flowers and a card tent with her name on it.

T.

My heart, my soul, the most important girl in the world. Simply put, I love you.

-Yours Always, Kaydy

She laughs but is also overwhelmed with tears of sincerity as he has already taken steps to romance her. He places their bags at the door as she runs up and jumps into his arms, peppering his face with kisses.

The force pushes him against the door, closing it with a slam. He is a bit shocked by her reaction as her hands start roaming his chest, inching their way lower. He holds her up with his strong arms, seconds away from losing control of his predatory urges. Phoenix is jumping at the bit to take over and make her his, he has to remind him of their plan.

"Baby doll, let's put our stuff away, I have everything planned out for us."

She stops and sighs, hops down, slightly disappointed. Teasingly, she grabs him and lets him go quickly and he responds by smacking her on the ass, she squeals as she grabs her smaller tote. He grabs the rest of their luggage and heads towards the bedroom.

She turns the corner to their bedroom and notices it has been set up in the most romantic way. There were rose petals everywhere and unlit candles for later.

He slides his hands around her waist, kissing her temple as she sighs. "Oh, baby...it's so beautiful. I've never had this done for me before, you're the best."

He opens her bag to put away her clothes into the closet, but she snatches a lace bag before he could see the contents and she quickly takes it into the bathroom with her.

The bathroom was equally romantic with rose petals, candles, and lots of bath beads and soaps in the corner of the whirlpool bathtub.

She notices two robes hanging nearby. A thick white cotton one, obviously for him, no guesses needed for the thin short red silk one.

"Now how do you know I won't be cold in this flimsy robe?" She yells out.

"Because I'll be doing everything in my power to keep you warm." He can't see her, but he knows she's blushing.

She tosses the lace bag between her hands; she needs a place to hide it until later. If he only knew the contents. Let's just say she was carrying a lot of Victoria's Secret.

"Everything alright in there, you took a bag, did you not need to unpack it?"

"Oh, it was just my toiletry bag."

He pulls out a bag full of bathroom stuff.

"Oh, I forgot I had two bags for the toiletries, you know, can't mix liquids with solids."

She began rambling off. He just nods and shrugs as he closes her empty suitcase and starts on his own, tossing his bag to her since she was at the door and she sets his toiletries on the right side of the double sinks. She preferred the left because she was left-handed, and it was closest to the door. Hey, she never said her logic made sense.

After unpacking and a much-needed nap after the long drive, Kayd proceeds to start the fireplace while she makes hot chocolate from scratch in the fully stocked kitchen. He had ordered everything they needed and more for their weekend.

She had showered and changed into a large flannel sleep shirt that fit her curves just right, it was more fitted than normal sleep shirts. Although she looked casual, she was wearing a pleasant surprise underneath. She shuffled in her tan knee-high socks and handed him his mug just as he was done stoking the fire.

He had taken off his shirt and was only in his black ripped jeans and barefoot, his hair slightly messy but beyond sexy. His smile lights up the room as he thanks her for the cocoa.

She sits next to him and snuggles into him after setting her mug on the table. She trails circles on his chest as he reaches back for the blanket covering the couch, wrapping them in it. She sighs as she feels her body temperature rise and not because of the extra layer. The crackling of the fire added to the seductive environment, fanning the flames of ecstasy.

"Have you decided what you want for dinner?" He looks down at her, noticing her eyes were closed but the constant movement of her fingers let him know she isn't sleeping, merely basking in their embrace.

"Mmm...surprise me, your choice, baby." He laughs while kissing her forehead.

Finding the remote to play some music while he decides what to make, he finds her favorite artist's station bringing a huge smile to her face.

She's singing unaware that he is paying attention, assuming he's wandering around the kitchen looking for ingredients.

He couldn't help but focus on her, her voice so soothing. She removed the blanket and walked to the sliding glass door while still singing, watching the darkness that is outside while sipping her cocoa.

Half an hour later, Kayd is finished making dinner which consisted of butter garlic glazed steak and fried plantains. He brought several bottles of his favorite wine, pouring each of them a generous amount.

"Oh my...I don't think I could eat another bite. Babe, you're the best." She sighs while tossing her napkin over her plate. He clears the table while she lies across the couch.

She closes her eyes but doesn't fall asleep, she lies on her stomach giving him a pleasant view when he returns to the living room.

He climbs on the couch kissing behind her knee, where the lace to her socks end, up to her thighs, eliciting a moan from her. He moves her shirt up to catch a peek of her bottom but gets a pleasant surprise when red lace underwear comes into view. She looks over her shoulder and winks as she hears a growl from his lips.

What he didn't know was that she had unbuttoned her shirt so that when she turned around in this moment, he would see her surprise.

He quirked an eyebrow as she flips over revealing a sheer, red lace bra and boy shorts.

As always, he starts growling and runs his hands through his hair, she brushes her foot across his lap, gauging his reaction.

"Sweet Moon Goddess, that is the sexiest thing I have ever seen, you have to stop wearing these things that make me want to pin you against the wall and steal your innocence." He eyes her like a piece of meat.

"Well, I guess tonight is your...lucky night, now isn't it? And you'll find out soon enough...I'm hardly innocent."

He pulls her up, she catches him staring at her half-naked frame and biting his lip. She coughs to grab his attention to her eyes.

"Umm yeah so I heard all of that...can't say I'm not impressed at your willpower at the moment if you are thinking like that."

She licks her lips seductively as he starts blushing, "I forget you can hear my thoughts, my uncensored thoughts. Sorry, love."

She shakes her head, "Don't be, I love when you think like that it's such a turn on. How about we take this to the bedroom so you can make love to me under the stars like you promised and all those other things you just thought." She jumps into his arms as he walks into their room.

After the most romantic night of her life, that included several rounds, they are soaking in the whirlpool tub surrounded by bubbles and candles. She lays against his chest and sighs, then tilts her head to meet his lips.

K: Wow, you were amazing...

Kayden: You do realize you aren't actually talking but thinking. I can hear your thoughts now.

K: I feel so connected and so safe with you...

Kayden: It also means that I can always find you if I need to and you can find me, I'll have to teach you how to put up a wall when you want your thoughts to yourself.

K: I wonder what else I'll gain from our romantic night

Kayden: I hope you don't think it's over, it's only midnight and I still have a lot on my mind

He gives her a devilish smirk as she stands to get out of the tub. He wraps her in an oversized towel and carries her to bed.

"Hey, I'm still naked!" He throws the towel to the other side of the room. "You're wearing exactly what you're supposed to..." She squeals as he attacks her with kisses and beyond...until the early hours of the morning.

The Letter

Early the next morning Kam starts to whimper as she aimlessly searches for him, her eyes still closed. She is jolted awake when she doesn't find him and just as she was about to get out of bed he walks in with breakfast.

"Morning, my love. I knew you'd miss me, so I whipped up a quick breakfast. I made pancakes, bacon, and fresh squeezed orange juice." He places the tray on her lap and he sits beside her.

"There's no way I can eat all of this, babe, you have to help me." She pours syrup all over and gives him the first bite. As he takes the bite, she removes the fork and gives him a quick kiss before cutting a piece for herself.

"I thought you said no kissing before your routine?"

She looks at him. "This, my dear, was the exception to the rule. Besides, you've completely spoiled me since we got here, and I wanted you to know how much I appreciate it."

He kisses her cheek and heads to the bathroom. "Oh, you haven't seen anything yet. Get dressed, we're going out on the lake today."

After a lazy day out on the lake, letting the boat wander aimlessly as they took in the beauty that surrounded them, they find themselves in a hammock on the porch facing the water. They couldn't entirely fit in the hammock together, so he has one leg out rocking them back and forth.

The sun was beginning to set when she brought out a plate of snacks so they could watch together. She brings out her wireless speaker to play some soft music as they watch the magical sunset before them.

She hugs him tighter. "You make me so happy; how did I get so lucky?" He looks down and sees her eyes watering, she wipes her eyes so that they don't fall on his tan henley, leaving spots.

He leans in to kiss her softly. "I'm the lucky one. You've stolen my heart since the first moment with you dancing around your shop to watching you light up when we're together, the way your dimples appear when I take your hand and the way you say my name when we're in the throes of passion. I am glad I waited for you, there's no one else for me."

He shifts to reach into his back pocket. He pushes up on his elbow as he pops open a box with the most stunning five carat diamond in rose gold setting. "Kamari Lee, will you spend the rest of your life with me? Be my wife, my lover, my supporter, and mother to my pups and I'll be everything you need, provider, supporter, loving husband."

The gasp took away her ability to speak for a moment. She gathers her breath once more, but the tears start to fall, and he tries to wipe them away, but they keep falling.

"Yes! Kayden James Miller, I would want nothing more than to be your wife!" He slips the ring on her shaking hand and they share a long, passionate kiss.

For the next three weeks, Kam has been training with both the pack and her mother, learning how to use her powers. She had become physically and mentally stronger and faster. Her runs to the falls were becoming too easy and now she was running at least five miles each time.

One morning, while conjuring with her mom, she instructs Brent to stand 100 yards away and wait for her instructions.

She calls Kayden over. "Babe, I need you to shift and run towards Brent. Don't flinch or stall, just full speed towards him, okay?" He looks at her quizzically then turns to look at Brent, who nods.

Phoenix emerges and immediately hits top speed towards Brent. Brent braces for the hit until he realizes he should have hit him by then, or so he thought. He opens his eyes; Phoenix was standing in front of Brent but because of her cloaking he could not see him. Brent looks at Phoenix but to him there was nothing there.

"Where did he go?!" He yelled back at Kam.

Kayden: I'm in front of you.

B: No, you're not, there's nothing in front of me

Kayden: I am literally standing in front of you, but you can't see me

K: And that gentleman is the power of cloaking, I hid Kayd from Brent. If needed I can cloak you from attackers and you can use it to your advantage. I also learned something else...

She un-cloaks Kayd and he appears right before Brent as he said. They both look back at Kam whose hair and eyes were violet, the wind began to whip her hair back as the storm clouds started to form out of nowhere, their anger in dark and thunderous form.

She reaches toward the sky and the lightning hits her but with no consequence, it was as if she was absorbing it. Once she had enough, her form crackled with electricity as she said a few words and directed her hands towards a tree and the lightning shot out and struck the tree, splitting it in half. Then the clouds parted, and his fiancée went back to her normal form.

Both guys had their mouths wide open. "Dude...do not piss her off, like ever."

Kayd shakes his head and jogs back up to her. Those training outside were amazed by the spectacle, it was known now of her status as a Legacy, being half wolf and half white witch, but this was the very first public display.

He wraps his arms around her, kissing her gently. "No offense, but that was so hot."

She busts out laughing, not expecting that response. "That was so smooth, who could resist such a line? Anyway, I am just glad my mom has taught me so much. I have one more hidden ability, but my mom says that because it is the dark magic that I'll only be able to execute in the moment, but I'll know exactly what to do. I hope I never have to use it." She sighs at the thought.

"I hope not either, but it is good to see you getting stronger both physically and in your powers."

Alpha, Beta, we've received a mysterious letter at the gate of the pack house. Come to the guard shack immediately!

The men take off towards the guard shack with Kam close behind. When they arrive, the guards are reviewing the tape to figure out how the perpetrator got near pack grounds and reached the gate.

"There's no one on the feed, it's like they knew where the surveillance blind spots were, but they left this specifically for you, Alpha Miller. We checked the surface for silver and wolfsbane, which came up negative.

Mark, one of the guards, hands him the small white envelope.

He cautiously opens it and reads it:

Your whole life is a lie, and I am coming to take what is mine, including her. Your days are numbered, and you don't have many left. I'll see you real soon. -JME

Sincerely, JME

After reading the message one more time over his shoulder, Kam stumbles back into the desk and her breathing becomes labored as if she'd seen a ghost.

No, it was far worse, a demon from her past was writing to her fiancé. She's on the verge of a panic attack.

Kayden roars loudly and violently balls up the paper. "I want security tripled around the border, I want a 24-hour detail for Kam, my mom, her business and her parents immediately. Kam, call Nessa and tell her to report to the pack house now!"

She doesn't respond except for the tears between her heavy breathing. She shakes her head in disbelief.

"No, no, no, no, just go away...just go away!"

He grabs her and his touch brings her out of her trance. "Do you know who it is? Tell me..."

She huffs and sighs. "It's obvious Kayd, JME...John Michael Evans, my ex wrote this."

Kayd's chest heaves up and down and his anger can't be repressed, it is written all over his face, his eyes darker than night and it actually terrifies her, she backs away from him, bringing him out of his rage because there's nothing more terrifying than him scaring her.

He pulls her to him and kisses her temple. "Don't be afraid, I'm sorry I let my anger get the best of me. I'm so sorry, baby."

She shakes her head, her eyes flashing violet.

"Un-fucking-believable! Every time I find a bit of happiness it gets ruined. I just thought..." Her shoulders slump and it's almost as if she's giving up.

She throws her hands up and walks away without another word. Her mother places her hand on Kayd's shoulder. "Let me talk to her." He reluctantly nods and her mother trails behind her.

His rage resurfaces. "I thought you had eyes on this bastard?! How the hell did he reach the damn front gate without being noticed, you're telling me no one could smell this rogue?!"

Frustrated, Kayd puts his fist through a wall, letting out a snarl.

"Find out what he meant! He's coming and I want to know why and with who and I want to know yesterday! I will not let him lay a finger on her, I'll skin him alive and castrate him myself. If he wants a war, he's fucking got it!"

Crying hysterically, Kam face plants on her bed. She didn't know how to handle this or what to do. What did he mean Kayden's life was a lie and he was coming for her? She made it crystal clear she wanted nothing more to do with him.

She didn't realize her mother was in her room until she brushed her hair away from her face.

"My sweet baby girl, you need to calm down. They will be ready for whatever is to come."

She sits up still crying profusely. "But it's my fault mom! John Michael has this weird obsession with me and I've made it clear that I don't want or need him. I love Kayd, my heart, my soul, it all belongs to him! But how can he love someone like me with so much baggage?"

Her mother soothes her by rubbing her back.

"Sweetie, I know we haven't been in your life, but you've always been well taken care of and Kayden loves you to the moon and back. He's going to fight for you, period. Doesn't matter if it's an ex, a rogue, or a whole pack, he's always going to be your knight in shining armor. The difference now is that you can help with the fight, I know he may not want you to, but you have powers that can help with whatever challenge is thrown at him. You've got to crawl out of this self-pity and continue your training, you are so much stronger than you look. Your union is blessed by the Moon Goddess herself, you, him and your children are meant for great things. You can do this, baby." They sit in comfortable silence for a while.

About an hour later, Kam didn't realize she had fallen asleep until she woke up in his arms and he's constantly kissing her forehead, whispering affectionate words in her ear.

Her tears reemerge as she remembers the events of the past few hours and she can't help but sniffle.

"Hey, no more tears. I'm going to fix this. No matter what, I'd die saving you, sweetheart. I love you so much. I don't want you to worry about anything, okay? You're mine and I'm yours, forever and a day."

He places a sweet kiss on her lips and she sighs. "How can you still love me after all this? I'm such a burden."

He shakes his head. "No, you are my angel and I love every inch of you, good and bad, just as I hope you would of me." They lock eyes.

"Of course I do, you're my entire world, I love you. I know you'll fix this; I just wish...you didn't have to."

He pulls her on his lap and places light kisses all over, paying special attention to her mark. Once he grazes her spot, she forgets the troubles of today.

"Ohhh, please..." She rocks against him as he pulls her shirt off and undoes her bra. He flips her on her back, kissing down her chest and stomach.

"Kayd, baby, please..." She begs once more as he kisses her stomach.

"What do you want, baby doll? Tell me..."

Once he reaches her underwear, she arches her back and bites her finger. "You...please, I need you." He smiles giving her all of him.

A while later he goes down to get them a snack as she puts on a movie so they can snuggle in bed. He comes back with popcorn, sodas, and a slice of cheesecake.

She takes a bite of cake and moans without regard to him staring at her, about five seconds from taking her again. She doesn't acknowledge but places a bite to his lips, he accepts it. "You're killing me, baby doll..."

Around 5 am, Kam stirs awake, his side empty. She puts on her robe and goes searching for him, he wasn't responding to her on link. She passes her armed security by her bedroom door.

"Paul, Riley where did he go?" She looks up at her humongous bodyguards who stood no less than six-foot eight inches.

"Good morning Luna, I believe he's in the basement gym." Paul radios her movement to the rest of the guards in the house.

There she saw Kayd hitting the punching bag, his entire upper body exposed and covered in sweat. He was hitting the bag pretty hard, obviously taking out his frustrations, combined with his grunts and growls. His headphones were in but that did not dull her scent.

"Why are you up?" He continues hitting the bag but doesn't look in her direction.

"You know I wouldn't be able to stay asleep. Besides, I know you're really upset by this and taking it out here. I wish this was never a problem..." Her gaze drops and he steps up to her, lifting her chin.

"I told you, stop blaming yourself. Besides, I needed to get back into my conditioning due to this upcoming whatever it is. I was hoping you wouldn't notice I wasn't there."

She scoffs, "Yeah the pile of pillows wasn't the same as you, they didn't snore like a wildebeest. How about I join you? My mom was right. I need to be physically and mentally ready, so you keep going and I'll be right back."

She went upstairs and returned in 10 minutes wearing a pair of biker shorts and a red sports bra.

When he notices her stretching before her run, he growls, pushing her against the padded concrete partition, kissing her roughly while his hands explore her body, pulling her legs up around his waist. Her breathing picks up as he pins her arms to her side and attacks her mark over and over, causing a whimper from her.

"Kayd...baby, this is not what I meant by exercise...oh...okay, you have to put me down."

He licks her mark eliciting another moan. "Do I? You say one thing, but your body tells me another."

She looks at him with a straight face. "Put me down, sir."

He huffs and sets her down. "Phoenix says you never let him have any fun." He goes back to the heavy bag and she starts running on the treadmill, after six miles she practices her cloaking spell aiming at a stationary bike facing the mirror.

She was learning how to evoke the spell as quickly as possible.

"Evictum morales hyperium!"

She screeched, causing a shield over the bike making it completely invisible.

She smiles as she realizes she's getting faster in memorizing the spells, but her mind wanders back to all the memories of John, they flood in like a dam breaking after torrential rain. She tries to shake them off but suddenly she's no longer in control...

Penelope

Her hair and eyes turn violet and the wind whips her hair around. She's not evoking a spell, she's reacting to all her anger and frustration at the moment, it had all gotten to her, the cheating, the lying, coming back to try to take her away from Kayd, it was all too much, and she had pent it up for too long. Even though she was not with him he still had this way of affecting her and she was sick of it.

Alpha, you need to come outside! There is a huge lightning storm and it's headed towards the house.

Before he could turn to stop her, she had disappeared, he ran outside. He sees her in the middle of the front yard. How did she get out here so fast? Can she teleport like her parents?

She was breathing heavily as the lightning began to increase in strikes, hitting the mountains near the property. She had lost control of her senses and the lightning was striking wildly.

"Kam, baby doll, listen to me, you have to calm down. I don't know how much damage you could inflict in your state right now. The storm is dangerous and heading towards the house, it could hurt someone. I need you to calm down sweetheart, please. You need to control your rage."

She turns around and looks at him, but he quickly realizes that it's not her but her witch.

"Control...my...rage?! Do NOT patronize me, I am not Kamari. I am Penelope, her white witch and I am in control to stop all the hurting. You don't have to feel the pain or the hurt or the guilt she feels, it's excruciating. All she wants is to be happy with you but then he comes and ruins it for her. He's threatening her happiness and I WILL NOT TOLERATE IT! I will do anything to end him and give her the happiness she deserves. You two are meant for so much more than to give this sad excuse for a werewolf the fucking time of day and when he comes, I will DESTROY HIS VERY EXISTENCE and if that whore is with him, then she's next."

She raises her hands and the lightning engulfs her, a ball of lightning floats above her hand and she directs it toward the mountain with all her energy while she shrieks. It slams against a metal satellite tower and completely destroys it causing a bright flash.

When he turns back to her, she is kneeling and panting on the ground. She brings her hands to her face then he cradles her in his arms.

"Kamari?" She sighs and nods as her hair returns to its curly state and he gazes into her signature eyes.

"I'm sorry, I'm so sorry I tried to tell her, but she was sick of feeling what I was feeling and took over."

She looks around and her eyes look up to the burning tower remnants on top of the mountain. "What have I done? I... I can't control her...I need to talk to my mom; she can help me."

Her eyes turn violet as she opens the link with her.

K: I couldn't control her mom, I- I don't know HOW to control her. What should I do?

M: Penelope has lain dormant for some time, but she has seen everything that has happened to you, she was essentially there, and she is not happy. She's going to seek revenge, she's your emotional outlet, I cannot guarantee you'll be able to control her when you see him, but you need to form a relationship to build trust, so she doesn't just take over again.

K: I was so scared! I could have hurt an innocent person.

M: That is one thing you never have to worry about, as a white witch you will not hurt the innocent and pure. We've only been practicing for a few weeks but you're just as powerful as I am and you're only meant to get stronger, you need to improve your relationship and let her know what you want.

K: Mom, will you be here when I do?

M: I'll be there around noon, baby. Get some rest until I arrive, that amount of power executed is very draining.

She shuts off the link to see a very concerned Kayden, he had been holding and rubbing circles on her hand.

"Baby, I'm so sorry, I shouldn't have bottled it up and made it seem like I was okay, I wasn't, I'm not. I am FAR from okay, I want to hurt him, and I want to hurt him bad. She knew that and she just snapped. My mom is coming to help me talk to her. I- I think I need to lie down; will you lay with me?"

He just nods as he presses his lips against her temple. She stops and looks into his green eyes.

"Do you still love me, despite what I am?"

"I love you BECAUSE of what you are and I'm not going to stop doing so, ever."
They head back into the house allowing her time to rest.

When her mother arrives, she suggests they occupy a confined space. Kayd suggests his painting room and asks his command to join.

Melody sits across from Kam.

"Are you ready? Just think of a place that soothes you and call her, she will come. I will be here if you need me."

She nods and looks at him. "I love you." He whispers it back as she closes her eyes.

She thinks about her apartment and is suddenly sitting on her couch. The sun warms the apartment from her bay window, she feels peace.

"Penelope?"

Her bedroom door opens and out walks someone who looks like her except has her violet eyes and hair.

"I assume you're here to talk about that little incident from earlier?" She sits and crosses her legs.

"No, Penelope, I owe you an apology. I should have expressed my anger, my feelings towards..."

She holds up her hand, her eyes flare and her hair whips around.

"DO NOT say that worthless bastard's name." She nods.

"*him*, instead I let it fester and I didn't realize how much you felt it. I know it's no excuse but I'm sorry. I know you only want to help but I need to be in control, I need to see this through but the moment I sense trouble I will call your name and give you control and you can finish this for us, for all of us, me, you and Tati. Deal?"

Penelope eyes Kam for a moment while conjuring up an electric ball.

"Deal, but once I get control I will not stop until he's wiped from this Earth! And that bitch, too."

They nod in agreement, although she hated violence it was clear he was not going to stop and she needed to protect her pack, her family, her love.

"Thank you for being my protector, I could not have asked for better than you and Tati." They share a final hug before she comes back to reality.

She shakes her head and blinks several times before she focuses back on everyone. She's smiling and it throws everyone off guard.

"She's agreed to give me control until I call her, after that it's literally his funeral."

Kayd hugs her as if she'd been gone for days, kissing her over and over. "I'm just happy to have my #1 girl back, we'll have to get you in the gym more to work out all that anger."

K: Or the bedroom...

She smiles but everyone groans.

Evan shudders, "Seriously, we ALL heard that." The guys walk out to avoid hearing much more, her mother chuckles.

Luna Ceremony

Her mother now focuses on all the artwork in the room.

"These are of Kamari, I can tell. These are beautiful, Kayden."

Tears well in her eyes as she studies each piece and even though her face is absent, she knew that beauty was that of her daughter.

"Aren't they, mom? He had dreamed of me and drawing his fantasies and I had done the same except I was drawing his wolf, Phoenix. We had been drawing each other until fate allowed us to be together."

She shakes her head as the tears fall. Kayd sees how emotional she is and makes a suggestion. "Mom, how about you take one for the townhouse? That way you always have a piece of her with you. Just take your pick and I'll have it delivered immediately."

That gesture causes her mom to wrap him up in a hug. The big bad Alpha was overwhelmed by his mother-in-law, which made Kam snicker but one look from him and she stopped. She decides to take the one of her on the beach. He has it wrapped and ready for transport.

Her mom leaves to promptly place it above their mantle.

Kam and Kayd take reprieve in their room. She sighs as she places her hand in his and admires the beauty of her engagement ring.

He breaks the silence, "The Luna ceremony is in three days, are you ready to make this official? It'll be the first full moon where you hold your reign."

She sighs, just the thought of it makes her stomach do flips. "Everyone has been so nice and understanding while I figure out just who I am and now I will officially be responsible for them and their well-being. Of course, I'm afraid, not only if I am good enough but of the unknown, all I want is for them to accept me."

He squeezes her to his chest. "They already accept you; they know what you are, and this is all a day to day thing. I went through the same thing when my father left the reign to me. You're going to be an amazing Luna and by my side I have the utmost confidence in us."

The harvest moon overhead, it's larger than normal size reflects pools over the beautiful ceremony stage awaiting the christening of a new Luna, a new beginning, and a stronger house.

Kam sits in front of her vanity checking her makeup. She had tried for the last hour not to cry.

"I am going to be a whole mess at our actual wedding."

She dabs her eyes with a handkerchief, she didn't want to disturb the fantastic makeup job her best friend created, she even added diamonds to accent her eyes. Nessa went with a bold eye with a nude lip.

"Oh, Nessa...I look breathtaking. You did such a great job, but why the nude lip?"

Nessa puts down the lip brush and smiles at her overly emotional friend.

"Because there is no need when you'll be sucking each other's face off and it would not look appropriate for the Alpha to have lipstick all over. What will his Queen think?"

Nessa winks, Kam shakes her head and laughs. She gives herself a once over in her silver one-shoulder, corseted waist gown. Nessa holds her up as she slips into her silver peep toe heels. The crown she was wearing was also silver, she looked like an Ice Queen. With her bouquet they open the door and her dad escorts her down the stairs and to the backyard where the entire pack of 700+ were waiting and her one...her love was waiting.

Once they stand at the mark for the ceremony to begin, she whispers, "Dad, I'm so nervous, what if they hate me? What if I..."

He stops her. "No, my beautiful girl, you are already royalty, you are worthy, and you will make this pack proud as their Luna. No more doubt, that man at the altar loves you more than the air he breathes. Focus on that and when you do it'll all fall into place. I love you, my princess." She nods, trying not to cry once again, and takes a deep breath as the doors open to the back yard.

She hears the gasps, but she focuses on the fairy lights strewn, dotting the surroundings like beautiful lightning bugs glowing a path to her forever.

Then her eyes meet his, the man who has loved her since the very moment he saw her.

Kayden stood in front of his throne waiting for her, he stood with the power and stature of a true Alpha King. He was slowly losing the battle as his breath hitches at the very sight of her.

Evan pats his shoulder, giving it a gentle tug. "You finally get your happy ending. Your brothers are beyond happy for you."

He smiles and nods, never taking his eyes off the angel walking his way. When Kam and her dad reach the end, much like in a wedding, her father kisses her cheek and Kayden steps down to take her hand. Once she is on the stage they turn to the crowd.

"Ladies and gentlemen, I present to you Kamari Lee, my mate and your Luna. Treat her with the same respect that you give me and love her as much as I do. Members of the Cheshire Pack please welcome her."

The whole crowd cheers loudly and there are whistles and thunderous clapping.

"Hear! hear! Welcome our Luna, our Queen!"

She receives a blessing from the pack priest and then she kneels in front of Kayden who places his sword on one shoulder then the other, confirming her title as pack Luna. He helps her recover before he places a long kiss on her lips and the crowd cheers.

He whispers in her ear. "Nobody is as happy as I am to have you as my Queen, I love you, baby doll."

She bows her head to him, accepting her new role and he escorts her to her throne.

She looks among the crowd to hopeful faces and general approval; the ceremony was now a celebration. He jars her out of her daze as he takes her hand and squeezes it lightly.

Suddenly there are shouts and screams as the crowd begins to part violently...an all too familiar voice calls out...

"A Luna should be married to a King and that man is no King! He is a fraud, he is not the rightful heir to the title of Alpha to the Cheshire pack, I am! As I am the *eldest* child of Mitchell Miller and I challenge you Kayden Miller for the title of Alpha!"

The crowd gasps as a figure comes through the middle of the crowd.

He sneers in Kayd's direction as his face is finally revealed. Kam gasps and shoots up from her throne.

"John Michael, what the hell are you doing here?!"

The Challenge

John finally sets his gaze on Kam and his jaw drops but it makes her feel dirty. His grin is sinister.

"You are absolutely still the most beautiful girl I have ever known, you look radiant as the new pack Luna, but I warned your little boyfriend I would come back for you, Kam. You were meant to be with me and no one else! I know I screwed up, but it was that mistake that forced me to find out who I was, how to be better for you and for us." He slowly approaches the stage. "My mom disclosed the details of her relationship with Mitchell, they spent two years together before he found his supposed mate, *his* mother, but she was already pregnant with me. She told him about me, but she decided to stay away, she didn't want to interfere with their fate and because of that she spent the rest of her life alone, she never found her mate and she died of a broken heart, watching her like that I vowed to never believe in that mate crap, she loved him, and he turned his back like a COWARD! Imagine my surprise when I found out that my love was your "mate", just another thing for me to take from you. I will destroy everything you have! I will not be without the one that I love most, mate or not, she belongs with me, and I will strip you of your title and your Queen!"

Kayden erupts from his throne, his crown crashing to the ground, his hair wild and disheveled from the forceful movement. It takes his entire command to hold him back, keeping a safe distance between the men.

"YOU?! You dare challenge me to the throne that is rightfully mine?! No pathetic bastard child that my father didn't even want will ever be enough for the throne let alone the love of my Luna, my wife! You speak of her again I will gladly gut you from neck to navel!" He continues to bear his teeth, growling in rage, Phoenix was coming into control.

Kam shoots up. "ENOUGH! I have had more than enough, I will NEVER be with you, I would rather die beside my husband than ever have you touch me again! You are beneath me, John Michael, a coward, a liar, and a cheater, far unworthy of the air you are breathing in the presence of my King. I have made it crystal clear that there is no us... take your leave and never return!"

He laughs. "Oh, I have every right...I may not be a full-blooded Alpha, but Alpha blood does run through my veins and it is my right to challenge my so-called little brother to the throne! You're going to see, I'm going to prove to you my worth, we WILL be together!"

She viciously shakes her head, whispering "No" before she becomes overwhelmed with emotion.

The pack priest steps through all the bodies separating the brothers, "If he is telling the truth,

194

then it is his right as a blood heir to challenge for the throne, Alpha Miller."

Kayden lunges forward as his command continues to struggle to keep him back, they add a few security guards to keep them apart. John just chuckles at his feeble attempt.

"How do we even know this miserable, worthless lowlife speaks the truth?! He lied to our Luna about his relations with another girl, how can we trust what he says now?! This pack will never accept you, look around, you are the enemy of all that witness you. They will NEVER accept you!"

"Oh, I don't need them to accept me little brother, it's you who wants their love and admiration but when I win, they will have no choice but to bow to me and follow my orders."

"Kayden...listen to me, please! He is telling the truth." He focuses on his mother's voice as it cracks at the anguish of revealing such a big secret so publicly, he turns to her but there is still much anger in his eyes. For the first time, she is in fear of her son as she has never seen him so enraged.

She places her palm to his face to calm him. "It's true. Your father did bear a son before he found me, he told me outright and I accepted it. The decision to keep it a secret was at the fault of both of us. I'm sorry son, but he is your brother."

John laughs, "Guess that makes you my EVIL step-mother. How selfish of you to keep a child away from his father all because 'fate' said you two were meant to be together but what about me? I was meant to be in his life too, guess what I want didn't matter, now did it?!" For a moment pain crosses his eyes before they fill back with rage and hatred.

The animalistic roars that leave Kayden's mouth are filled with violence and fury; they are inhuman.

"You will watch your words when you speak to my mother! You are NOT my brother and it is of no consequence if I kill you where you stand!"

Kam is battling on the inside, doing her best to control both Tati and Penelope, they had agreed to not interfere until they were called but that was before this and Tati was chomping at the bit to clamp down on his throat and end it quickly. Penelope was so quiet it was beyond frightening, she had reached a level of madness that would scare the devil himself, but she reigned herself in, as promised, the internal battle was causing her body to physically shake.

Kayd still has his sights trained on John, his eyes the blackest of black. Phoenix was infuriated and wanted blood, he wanted more than blood, he wanted his soul for interrupting such a wonderful event and upsetting his Queen.

His Queen who was now in his view and urging him to look at her.

K: My King, please... this is what he wants, he wants to distract you, use your anger against you. Look at me, NOW Kayden James!

His eyes slowly focus on hers. His breathing calms as he feels the tingles from her touch, her eyes are filled with tears. He sighs deeply as he wipes her tears. He notices how badly this was affecting her, he holds her hands tighter to calm the shaking.

He holds her close which seems to lessen the shaking.

"You want to challenge me for the throne, for the title of Alpha of the great Cheshire Pack? I accept, *brother*..." The last word emphasized, practically spitting acid.

Turning on his heels, Kayden stops. "Tomorrow night, a fight to the death...you won't get another chance."

He takes Kam's hand and they head toward the pack house while security escorts John off the premises. He had come seemingly alone but they were smart enough to know he was not alone at all; he was a rogue and probably had a pack who followed his command. Security would be heightened immediately until after the fight, they would have to dip into their ready reserve to cover the grounds and key members of his family.

"Run...little brother! Enjoy your last night with her, she will be mine! She has always been mine and no one will get in my way!"

It is deadly silent after John gets the final word until they reach his office. Evan, Brent, Miles, both of their mothers and Kam await his initial reaction.

The men flank the women, not chancing his reaction to everything that just occurred.

He gives them more than they bargained for when he flips his solid mahogany desk with a loud roar.

He pulls at his hair as a coping mechanism before putting his fist through the wall, he was obviously not coping well. He starts pacing a path into the ground.

"Why, mom?! Why would you and father keep this secret from me? A brother, a bitter brother who happens to be the jealous determined ex of my wife! He's threatening to take her from me and family or not I will dismember him, he means nothing to me, blood will not keep me from destroying his very existence. She is worth fighting and dying for."

He takes a moment to look out the window and sighs. "You know what honestly bothers me... is that someone like him had her first." He starts pacing once more.

Kam had heard and seen enough, she picks up her dress and stands directly in his path, he has no choice but to stop before her.

Her eyes are flashing between violet and her natural color. "Tati is fuming but Penelope is maintaining radio silence and that scares me more, I am not sure what she is capable of, I can barely contain her, our spoken agreement means nothing after this drama. And as far as I'm concerned, he may have had me first, but you have me forever. He was many firsts, the first to cheat on me, the first to lie to me and the first to break my heart. There is no need to be jealous my King, I am yours, always."

Her eyes flicker once more and it concerns him just how upset his brother made her.

He places his hand on her cheek, looking her in her eyes, past Kam and into Penelope.

"Penelope, please, let me take care of this. It is my duty as Alpha to fight and protect her. If at any point I need you she will summon you, but right now give her control, conserve your energy."

He presses a kiss to her forehead and he feels her physically relax. When he looks at her, her eyes are filled with tears, she can't stop her emotions from flowing over.

"This is insane, my ex is challenging my King for his crown and the best part?! It gets better... They're BROTHERS! How fucked up is my life right now? And you know he's going to try every dirty trick in the book to gain it. FUCKING HELL!" She paces with one hand on her hip and the other on her head.

He tries to pull her in, but she slaps his hands away.

"Don't! And I can't believe you challenged him to the death! What if something happens...if he wins, I-I'll die." Her breathing becomes rapid as her mother does her best to keep her steady, she's seconds away from a breakdown.

"Kamari, I'm sorry, I reacted out of emotion. I love you and it is my duty to protect you, protect my pack, the people who expect me to keep them safe. Please understand why I did what I did."

She was still fuming when he stepped right up to her, no smile no nothing, just gazing into her eyes.

"I need time to center myself and focus, we will be in the gym prepping but I will be up later to wrap my arms around you as we fall asleep together officially as Alpha and Luna, I will not let him ruin the best night of my life so far, confirming you as my Luna, as my Queen. I look forward to 43 days from now when you will legally be my wife and I, your husband."

He kisses her softly, placing one lastly, on her forehead. "Trust me, baby, please."

She nods reluctantly under her tears and he wipes her cheek.

"I want you to do everything it takes to rid us of him forever, I need you Kayden...*we* need you..."

Surprise

There is a collective gasp then the entire room falls silent and Kayd's eyes widen as they make their way lower.

"Really...a baby? How could I have missed this? I was so angry it must have dulled my senses and I didn't pick up on it..." His tears slip so easily this time as he falls to his knees.

She runs her finger through his hair, her tears flowing like water.

"You have to fight for us, your wife... and your child. I can't do this alone." She rubs her stomach as he gently places a kiss on it.

Both their mothers hug her tightly, squealing. Nessa's hand is over her mouth in complete shock.

"When were you going to tell us?"

She shrugs her shoulders "It was going to be at the culmination of the ceremony, or it was supposed to be."

Her mother is all smiles despite the situation, "And now that we know this, you will be the most powerful pack in the world when the baby is born, but the power is already in you. The powers of the mother doubles exponentially as she carries the powers of said child. It is a transference of energy; all of your spells will be twice as powerful."

He shakes his head. "No, I do not want you anywhere near the battle, I have to keep you and our baby safe."

"You're out of your damn mind if you think I'm agreeing to that! If I need to help you I will Kayden, that's that!"

He takes her hands and kisses them as his forehead rests against hers.

"At least we know the baby will be twice as stubborn as its parents." A laugh rings through the room.

He nods, "Fine, but I want you in the sky box. The moment you sense something wrong I want you to call Penelope, I know she will keep you safe in any way possible."

She nods in agreement as he kisses her once more. "I can't believe it! I love you...and you, too, little one."

He leans down and presses a kiss to her stomach.

"And we love you, daddy."

He changes clothes and the men head down to the gym to come up with a battle strategy.

"This is serious, it will be a no-holds barred fight to the death, there will be a referee to officiate the match. I agree with Kam, he is going to try any and everything. From what I found out, John Michael

Evans left town and settled in nearby Prattsville, about 250 miles north of here. While there he became head of the rogues of the North pack, the same ones we found at our border weeks ago, probably staking out the territory. We estimate about 50 other rogues follow his lead. We have completely revamped protocol and will have essentially three rings of security with me and Brent guarding Kam. Evan will be ringside with you to ensure a fair fight."

Kayd nods at the information while hitting the punching bag with full force, his external facade was calm while he was raging on the inside. The only reason the bag was not punched to the other side of the gym was Miles leaning against it, but he still felt the blows. Kayd's strength had definitely increased over time since they mated and the anger only enhanced it.

"Our entire pack is still here so we will use the amphitheater to house them. After tonight's ordeal no one is leaving you, they are here to support and fight if need be. Their loyalty is to you." Kayd nods as he belts out a series of combinations.

Evan clears his throat, apparently, he was in charge of relaying the last bit of information.

"One last thing, Kayden..."

He used his whole name, that was not a good sign, he could feel his jaw tense up.

Evan runs his fingers through his hair, the subject was sensitive and would cause him to flip out.

"after John broke off his engagement to Bridget, he took her back when he went rogue, taking her along with him but he failed to tell her his true intentions with Kam and he formally rejected her, she flipped out and vowed to destroy both of them and she hasn't been seen since. I have a bad feeling she's going to show up and try to hurt Kam and now that we know she's pregnant..."

Kayd snaps the bag off its pedestal and climbs on top wailing on it as if it's John, he roars as he hits a left then a right, his speed ruthlessly fast. The bag essentially bursts due to the force of the hits and sand pours everywhere.

"You find her! If she lays a finger on Kam, I will crack her windpipe between my teeth and claw her heart out!"

Upstairs, Kam was still trying to reach Penelope.

K: Penelope, please, talk to me... I know you're pissed just let me know you're there and that you will let me lead tomorrow?

P: I am fine. I am doing what our mate says and am conserving my energy but know that when you call on me, and you will, I will not hesitate using black magic. He'll never see the light of day again and he will suffer tremendously before he dies.

With that Penelope cut off their link.

"Shit..."

Around 2 am Kayd tiptoes through their bedroom to the bathroom for a much-needed shower.

He had spent an hour going over strategy, another working out his frustration, and the last hour in meditation.

The hot water never felt so good as it did now, his muscles were sore, but the temperature of the water was ice cold compared to the hatred coursing through his veins.

Finally, he says a prayer to the Moon Goddess to protect himself and his growing new family.

He can't help but smile as he reflects on these past few weeks. Kam had been sick for a while now, not being able to keep anything down and she was always taking naps in the middle of the day, claiming she was just exhausted.

She blamed it on all her training, or a cold or maybe something she ate but she was wrong...she was pregnant... pregnant with their first pup.

He wondered if her Legacy powers kept him from smelling it on her. She was still a walking mystery and now would have to be observed to see how pregnancy affects her powers.

Even through this whole despicable ordeal he smiles, she was carrying their world and soon he would be a father.

He steps out of the bathroom in just a towel, walking toward their closet to grab a pair of pajama pants.

"Mmm...don't even bother, I need my King to make love to me."

He turns to see her sitting up, wearing a black silk slip that barely covered anything. One strap had slipped off her shoulder and she was playing with the other seductively.

"You wouldn't believe how much being pregnant makes you needy all the time. Like ALL the time, so what do you say?"

She runs her fingertips all over causing her to moan in response.

The way she responded, and her moans caused all his blood to rush south as he growled, and she bit her finger waiting for him to pounce and he did.

After he effectively satisfies all her desires, he wraps his arms around her and kisses her shoulder repeatedly. "I really can't believe you're pregnant, I thought you were on birth control. Why couldn't I smell it on you?"

She lies on her back looking him in the eyes caressing his jaw line.

"My mom told me that birth control is useless to Legacies, of course it is, she also says to keep the child safe the scent is masked from everyone including the mother, she can only rely on the basic symptoms that humans encounter, hence the morning sickness, aches, and of course, missed period. I took a pregnancy test and confirmed with the pack obstetrician."

Kiss & Makeup

There's an uncomfortable moment of silence between them.

"I'm so terrified, Kayd. I don't trust John Michael, he's deceitful and this outburst tonight confirms he is desperate to carry out this crazy plan of his no matter what. And there is something very off about him, I can't place it, but something is definitely not right."

He takes her hand and kisses it as she continues, "He doesn't want to rule out of adoration, this is pure unadulterated spite, to cause as much damage as possible, he is literally trying to take down the entire pack and is using our situation for his gain."

He nods confirming her fear. "I know, I felt it the moment he challenged me. His obsession with you fuels him and when it comes to loving a woman, you're willing to do anything."

She scoffs, sitting up slightly. "Love? He never knew what that was, whatever he thinks this is, it definitely isn't love." She rolls her eyes heavy at the very thought.

Kayd pulls her close, staring into her eyes trying to read her.

"Tell me, did you love him?"

She pulls away harshly, reacting angrily to his question.

"Did I love him? Are you seriously asking if I loved the man who made me feel completely worthless, broke my heart, and caused me to feel a pain like no other? Hmmm, let's take a wild guess, shall we?! Hell no, I did not love John Michael. We weren't even together three months before the incident, that wasn't enough time."

He looks shocked.

"But you loved me after a week..."

Her body jerked in reaction; her head tilted to one side to make sure she heard what she thought she heard. All traces of breath left her body, it came out as a strained cough. Her face fell into shock that quickly evolved into anger.

"Are you fucking kidding me?! Really?! You want to compare my forever relationship with you to my situation-ship with John Michael? You, 'my darling husband', can kiss my ass! There isn't even a comparison and you, Kayden James Miller, will not stress me out and put our baby in harm's way with your fucking pity party. How dare you?! Find someone else to be your damn punching bag, you're playing right into what he wants, to separate us, to cause pain and harm so congratulations on doing just that...prick..."

Oh, she was pissed, but she was right. Her tears are flowing as Nessa doesn't wait for permission, she barges right in.

"What the hell is going on? I can practically hear you from my room downstairs! Kayd, why is your pregnant fiancée in tears? Somebody better answer me this minute, my witch is already at level ten and is just itching to come out." Nessa's hair shifts between its natural color and silver.

Kam hugs Nessa and Nessa glares at Kayd.

Realizing the unnecessary pain he put her through he falls to the ground against the bed, as if in prayer, he needed her forgiveness, he couldn't believe what he said.

"How could I say something so stupid, baby I'm so so sorry, for a split second I was scared he meant something to you still even after all this. I can't lose you, you're all I have and you're carrying my world within you. I let my fear get the best of me and I took it out on you, I'm sorry, my love. Please, forgive me, please...I can't win without you. I admit it...I am weak without you by my side."

He looks up to see her sitting beside him, his tears flowing. He was allowing John to win emotionally.

"Look at me... you cannot let him win already; we are stronger than this. Tomorrow I want you to fight for what you love, he can never have what you have, and I want you to show him, the pack, and his followers that YOU are indeed the true Alpha King. I know you didn't mean what you said but it still hurt. You owe me more than just an apology."

He nods as she wipes his tears while he holds her waist laying his head in her lap. She smiles and laughs as he places kisses on her belly.

"You know, if you stay down there you might as well..."

"OH DEAR GOD, why am I always here to hear things like that, okay all is well I'm going to go now. UGH... I both love and hate you two. Goodnight!" Nessa makes a beeline for the door.

Kayd looks up at her and is in love all over again as she places her hand on his cheek, her touch calming to his nerves. He takes her hand and they cuddle on the bed, talking about all they are thankful for and before they go to sleep, he makes love to her again.

It's 8 am when Kam shifts around to wrap her arms around him, nuzzling her face into his chest and inhaling deeply.

He reacts warmly to her touch. "Every morning you do this is the best feeling ever. Good morning, baby doll."

He kisses her forehead not quite opening his eyes as he rests his chin on top of her head, running his fingers up and down her back. She shifts her body to lay across him as she sighs.

"Morning, I hope you remember what I said last night."

"You mean when you were moaning my name at that pivotal moment? I'll never forget how my name sounds from those gorgeous lips of yours, if you say it now, I might just lose it."

His entire body shudders as her eyes fly open and she gives him a dirty look. He gives her his prize-winning smile and suddenly she's putty in his hands.

"You know what I mean. Today is about finishing what he started, and I know you can, no doubt, no fear, just the confidence within you to fight for your family and your pack."

He nods as he inhales her scent deeply, which calms him tremendously. He rubs her belly for comfort and she giggles because she is barely showing.

"So how about we have the kitchen staff bring up breakfast this morning? I just want to lay with you all morning."

She agrees and calls down to have their breakfast brought up. About twenty minutes later there was a knock at the door as one of the servants brought it to their bed.

"Thank you, Wendy, you're an absolute doll." Kam says as she smiles at all the food she ordered laid on their bed. She was already craving weird combos such as spaghetti and mashed potatoes, cream cheese and jalapenos, and her favorite, orange juice with lemonade.

Kayd eyes her choices next to his traditional breakfast and quirks an eyebrow. "O...k this is going to be one long and strange pregnancy."

She eyes him as she gleefully digs into the spaghetti and mashed potato combo. She sighs in fat kid bliss as she scoops some cream cheese onto a slice of jalapeno.

"Umm, sweetie, is that safe to eat, it's spicy." She grins as she pops it into her mouth.

"I am carrying the most powerful being in the world and what baby wants, baby gets. And baby wants daddy to mind his business and let mommy enjoy her food."

She smiles to ease the snarkiness and leans forward for a kiss, which he happily obliges disregarding the heavy taste of cream cheese on her lips.

After their meal they snuggle for a while before he has to break away to take a shower and get to the gym for a last-minute training session and meditation.

Ready for War

T he skies were darker and more ominous than normal tonight, filled with anger and rage, threatening to pour at any moment if they were real thunderstorm clouds but they weren't. These were conjured up by the hatred that coursed through Kam's, rather Penelope's, veins.

The amphitheater was to capacity but there were overflow locations to accommodate the rest.

The crowd was restless, talking about this stranger who threatened Alpha Miller's reign and the shocked faces when they found out their relation.

Eyes wandered up to the Royal box to watch every move that Kam made. Would they hate her because of the past mistake she made in dating the older brother of her mate? She didn't know him or the mating process, and it wasn't as if she had any feelings now except pure hatred.

Kam began feeling restless on her throne awaiting to see her love. She has Miles and Brent flanking behind her guarding the royal entrance to the box. Their eyes darted all around not leaving a second to chance.

"Despite your apprehension, Kam, they are only loyal to you and Kayd. You needn't worry about your pack." She gives him a small smile.

215

Suddenly, the crowd parts with loud thunderous boos and jeers as John steps forward, more confident than before. He's also a lot more muscular than the time she saw him in her shop, he was dripping with cockiness as if he had already won.

He demanded his 'pack' be allowed to watch near the ring, Kayd reluctantly accepted preparing a section for them to stay together, not allowing them to wander around pack grounds; they were always watched by his security. Each floorboard where their feet were was pressure sensitive so if someone left, they would trigger a silent alarm. Having rogues on the premises was unheard of unless they were in the dungeon to be tortured, then killed, which is what he planned when he won the match. Kayd didn't want to chance them sneaking into the territory while the fight was happening, who knows what damage they could cause. At least he had them contained and after he would dispose of them all.

John's eyes look up at Kam and she feels uneasy. He bows to her and she shifts her eyes away from his gaze.

"My Queen, do not ignore me for soon it will be you calling me your King and I will be ruling these mangy flea-bitten mongrels."

She addresses him with fire in her eyes. "I will NEVER be with you John Michael, stop this absurd challenge and take your pack of rejects and leave me!" Her comment only angers him more.

"Then I have no choice but to rip your KING apart and make you watch as he bleeds out before me and when you realize you have nothing you will have no choice! No imaginary mate bond is stronger than my love for you Kamari, you will fall before me."

She shudders at the sound of her name; how could she have been so stupid as to fall for someone like him? He makes her sick to her stomach.

Suddenly the trumpets blare signaling Kayd's arrival to the ring. He looked calm and centered, not a doubt in his mind. He looks in her direction and nods, he couldn't help but notice the uneasiness in her face.

Kayden: Do not worry my love, I am ready for this, ready to end this once and for all. He will not get everything I've worked so hard for.

K: Please be vigilant, my love, I don't trust him at all.

Kayden: I know. Once the fight starts, I will cut off our link, I need no distractions to give him an upper hand, forgive me. I love you, baby doll.

She sighs, holding back her tears.

K: I understand, just know that we love you very dearly.

He looks at her and bows to her, blowing her a kiss, she mouths to him 'I love you' as he makes his way. He then focuses his attention back on his brother, who snarls at his presence.

"What's wrong big brother, upset that I have the one person you cannot have? Her heart belongs to me and more importantly she is carrying my child...looks like at best you'll be an uncle."

He smirks, laughing, while relaying that bit of information. John only sees red as he lunges forward but the referee stops him allowing Kayd to earn the first point in mind games.

The official covers the rules, including that when one opponent shifts the other must as well unless they are too injured to do so. If they cannot shift, they are deemed unfit to continue with the fight and must forfeit. The referee is the only person who can stop the fight and has the final decision.

The bell rings, causing immediate anxiety in Kam.

John and Kayd dance around trying to avoid each other's grasp until John gets a hold of Kayd's arm and pins it behind his back and John's arm is across his chest. Kayd uses his leverage to flip John, which was no easy task as he was only slightly taller but just as strong as Kayd without the Legacy power boost.

The revelation caught him off guard for a moment, just enough for John to land two powerful blows to his jaw. Kayd stumbles back to the edge of the ring, wiping the blood and smiling, spitting out some blood to the floor. Kayden charges full speed towards his brother burying his shoulder in his abdomen, ramming him into the ground with great force, knocking the air out of his lungs. John lies there stunned by the force of the slam and his brother's strength.

His pack members were screaming for him to get up, to not let the 'pretty boy' win and that the title was rightfully his.

Kayd takes no chances in giving him any time to recover, landing blow after blow to his body and he only laughs as they do not seem to affect him. He switches tactics and goes for his jaw and nose, breaking both with such force, he was not laughing now.

However, he was still strong enough to shove Kayd off him and clear across the ring, Kayd's eyes widened in shock. He watches as he straightens out his nose and relocates his jaw as if it were nothing.

Kam watches in fear but also in curiosity. "Something isn't right Brent, he should be feeling some pain or reacting, but he's not, it's like an adrenaline rush or..."

Miles walks to the edge of the box, narrowing his eyes. "He's been taking enhancers, for who knows how long. He's got all the symptoms of steroid use and even with your Legacy powers, Kayd's still getting beat out there."

When she looks back Kayd is flat on his back taking a series of merciless punches until John shifts into his wolf. He is all black with piercing blue eyes except for a white ring around his right eye, the exact opposite of his brother!

He paces around waiting for his little brother to shift. John snarls, ready in a pounce position.

Kayd finally shifts and Phoenix tilts his head noticing the similarities until John's wolf lunges towards him, teeth bared only millimeters from his neck and for a second Phoenix whimpers. He was completely overpowered and for a second, he feared he would lose everything.

Kam was so preoccupied with the match she didn't hear the grunts and two thuds behind her until it was too late. She whips around to see Brent and Miles on the floor unconscious with darts in their back. She stands up quickly realizing there was nowhere to go, and that Evan had also turned off his link to focus on John and his group.

"So, the whore thinks she can have the throne...when my beloved rightfully takes his place?"

Kam sighs loudly, thoroughly irritated, not even needing to turn around to figure out who the mystery voice is. She whips around to see Bridget.

"I don't know what it is about you people interfering where I don't want you. What do I have to say to get it through your head that I don't want John Michael, take him and leave my pack grounds, you're not wanted here!"

Bridget brandishes a knife. "Oh, but you see it's not that simple. John is obsessed with you, he thinks you're his one, and the only way to win him back is to eliminate you from the picture so I can have him all to myself and that's what I plan to do. He'll beat that pathetic excuse for a brother and take his place and once you're gone, I will reign as Queen!"

Bridget Meet Penelope

She takes a step forward as Kam takes one back. She slides the knife across her tongue, menacingly.

"How does someone pathetic and weak like you have two brothers fighting over your love down there? They are willing to die just to have you on their arm. What makes you so special, huh? What makes you better than me?"

Kam can feel both Tati and Penelope stirring just at the sight of her, it was in her best interest to leave but she knew she wouldn't and as Penelope said, "she would be next". The angry clouds are increasing around them, lighting up the sky in fury.

Bridget takes another step forward. "ANSWER ME!"

Kam jumps at her shouting and although she should feel threatened by a crazed woman brandishing a knife she does not and she responds calmly.

"What makes me better than you, Bridget? It's simple...I know my worth, I'm not sleeping with every man in sight, all probably because daddy didn't love you, huh? Typical. That's probably why you went along with the proposal because you wanted to please daddy and then you found yourself actually liking your mark but when he realized he was scraping the bottom of the barrel, he bailed, twice now, right? While all I wanted was a stable and steady relationship, I wanted my forever love and for a split second I stupidly thought that was John, but any man who is willing to slum it up with you is no man I want. If he wanted it easy, he could have just said so. I'm glad that all this happened because if it hadn't, I wouldn't be with the *better* brother, I wouldn't be Luna to this mighty pack, and I wouldn't be carrying his child...right now."

Phoenix found a way to get back on all fours. He watches his brother circling him, he has to be smart about every move.

He was doing this for her and his future family she was carrying, and no one was going to come in between him and their happiness. John lunges at him once more and this time is able to plunge his teeth into his shoulder and bite down viciously the sound of bones cracking echoed throughout the amphitheater. Phoenix lets out a soul piercing howl as he collapses to the ground whimpering. The crowd falls eerily silent.

Kam turns around after hearing Phoenix howl in pain.

"No! Phoenix!"

She doesn't notice Bridget coming behind her holding the knife just a hair away from her neck.

"Let's watch shall we and then I'll enjoy watching you bleed as John watches me prove just how much I love him enough to eliminate his little obsession."

Kam's breathing is irregular as tears form in her eyes watching Phoenix bleed, not even concerned for her own well-being.

Phoenix limps around as John shifts back to his human form. He laughs maniacally, raising his hands as if he had already won, his section cheers for him proudly.

"What's wrong *little* brother, unable to shift due to all the pain? I guess that means you lose to me, say it! Admit who is the rightful King of this pack! The last thing you will see is me claiming your Queen, she was quite the screamer in bed."

Phoenix looks up and he shifts back to his human form, his shoulder and chest is covered in blood and the bite marks are slow to heal. His anger has reached another level as he talks about harming her and that was the last straw.

"I will NEVER concede to a despicable, disgusting excuse for a werewolf or a man, I will die protecting my family and my pack!"

John cracks his knuckles.

"Then so be it...brother." In a split second a member of his pack throws him a blade and he quickly grabs it, setting his sights on Kayd.

"No!"

Kam screams again. Bridget tightens her grip and presses the knife further onto her neck.

"Looks like the end for your precious Alpha and we've got the best view in the house."

Kam closes her eyes.

K: Penelope, I need you. I must protect our child. Please help our Alpha, my love. Finish this...

P: My Queen, realize once you release me, I will do any and everything to rid us of this infestation, it will not be pretty. I plan on making them suffer.

K: I know. You can take control...

Bridget is pushed back by some unknown force until she slams against the wall to the entrance, she is frozen in fear as Kamari's hair turns bright purple, cascading down her back and shifting in the wind. She turns around and her eyes are glowing violet.

Bridget tries to escape and put as much space between them, but Kam holds her hand out, shielding her exit.

"Now where are you running off to? Stay... and let's watch the show, shall we? I've been itching to get my hands on you since you decided to whore yourself out to Kam's man, who turned out to be shit too. Doesn't matter...he still wasn't yours to take. Now, how can I torture you today? So many great options..."

An evil smile forms across Penelope's lips, her mouth practically watering at the revenge she finally gets to carry out.

Bridget's mouth is wide open as she tries to form a coherent sentence.

"Wh-what are you? You're... not normal."

The clouds begin to form about putting on a spectacular light show.

"You're right, I am not normal, far from it. I'm a lot of things, I'm a lover, an artist, but most importantly to you, WE are your worst nightmare Bridget, and nobody can save you...you made a mistake by coming back, a fatal mistake."

Penelope looks down at the ring just as John's cohort throws him a blade and she quickly waves a force field between them; she whips her finger and the knife flies out of his hands and out of his reach before the force field subsides.

Penelope focuses back on Bridget who has nothing but fear in her eyes.

"You see, Bridge, is it okay if I call you that? Doesn't matter....you see, Bridge, you have THE absolute worst luck in picking your enemies. I bet you thought Kam was just some timid little push over. You'd be able to get away with blowing her boyfriend and she would just fold. Well, she did, and you won. Little did your whorish mouth know that it was ME who pushed her to find you two together...why? Because she is of royal Legacy blood, a Princess, destined to be with someone who is commanding, strong, and willing to sacrifice everything for her. Your precious John Michael isn't fit to spit on."

Bridget laughs in her face. "You're a liar! All Legacies are dead! You're just pathetic. It was so nauseating how everyone loved you and you were the town sweetheart. It sickened me to know you were soooo perfect that I had to find a flaw in your innocent persona so yeah, I enjoyed your reaction when you saw me with John, just as I was finishing him off for the *third* time. He loved it, he knew I was so much better than you in bed and that's why he came to me. He's going to be Alpha and he's going to be mine and there's absolutely nothing you can do about it! I am going to destroy you, Kamari!"

Now it was Penelope's turn to laugh.

"Oh sweetie...Kam's not here now, didn't you hear me when I said we? You really should stop doing drugs, sweetie... I suppose you should formally meet the one who's going to cause you to take your last breath, please...call me Penelope..."

She jokingly holds out her hand for a handshake. When she doesn't reciprocate Penelope just shrugs her shoulders nonchalantly.

John looks stunned as he no longer has the upper hand.

"What just happened?!"

Kayden smiles. "My wife just happened; you see John there was a reason you weren't meant to have someone as unique as her. Kamari is Princess to the Violet Legacy line; she is meant to be with a leader not some pathetic unloved bastard child! You had the most kind and loving woman and what did you do, ha, you made it easy for her to love me brother, so thank you."

John shakes his head. "You're lying, all the Legacies were wiped off the map long ago, there are none left."

Kayd smiles as the lightning flashes around them. "Well, that's where you are wrong, the power of the Legacy blood flows within her and our baby. You're going to regret stepping foot on my pack grounds."

John Michael is stunned to see the long violet locks that now grace her back and glowing eyes to match.

"Oh Bridget, it is I who will be destroying you and your little boyfriend, too. Never speak Kamari's name as long as you live, which, luckily for you won't be much longer."

Penelope's eyes glaze over making them completely white and her skin covered in black vine markings as she recites the spell she would execute if necessary.

It was black magic but to save her baby and her King she had no choice and allowed Penelope to carry out the spell. Kam takes a deep breath and allows herself to sink deep into her subconscious as Penelope recites the spell.

With the wind whipping around, Penelope reaches up and the lightning makes contact from the clouds into her being, the lightning hovers as a ball above her hand but then she recites another incantation and the ball turns into bright blue flames.

Her lips curl up into an evil smirk just as she hurls the ball in Bridget's direction with a soul shattering screech, grabbing the attention of all below.

The flames swirl around Bridget, leaving her untouched until Penelope snaps her fingers and the flames engorge her, Bridget instantly lets out the most painful wails before falling to the ground.

The crowd gasps at what they just saw.

John stands there in utter shock, all the rage boils over and he pummels a distracted Kayden to the ground. He took joy slowly taking the very existence of his brother.

The fact that Bridget made Kam's life insufferable didn't mean she deserved to die in that way.

"I'll kill you!" He slams Kayden down repeatedly on his head until he almost loses consciousness.

"Penelope..." He whispers out, his eyes fluttering and fighting to stay open.

Penelope appears in the ring, the lightning to ground strikes signaling her presence as the wind swoops forward.

John jumps off of Kayden. "But...h-how did you?" She tilts her head, hair whipping back fiercely as her anger grows.

She tsks.

"Oh John Michael, not only did you try to take everything away from Kamari, but you tried to cheat in the process. I can smell the stench of wolf steroids on you. Let these be the last words you hear before you die just...like.... Bridget. You mean nothing to her, less than nothing, and your brother is the far better choice! She's SO much better without you and I hope you realize just how much you screwed up."

The fear in his eyes meant nothing to her, she had tried to let him walk away but he and Bridget simply refused, so they had to die.

"Kamari, please..."

She snaps in his direction. "You will address me as Princess Kamari Lee of the Violet Legacy, Luna to the great Cheshire pack, and wife to Alpha King Kayden Miller. Goodbye John Michael...and good riddance..."

His eyes widened and she held both hands into the sky letting the lightning gather around her before she recites the spell again but this time her entire being is engulfed in flames. Finally, she directs everything in his direction. All her hurt, her pain, her anguish with the ordeal.

He immediately falls to the ground screaming, but his death is excruciatingly long until there is silence.

Before they can react to the horror they saw, she sets her sights on his pack and uses the force field to trap them and sends another fire-ball in. All that could be heard were screams of pain and agony until...there wasn't.

After the ordeal, Kam collapses to her knees, head in hands, breathing rapidly. Kayden runs to her and hugs her tight.

"Kam, baby doll, are you alright? Talk to me!" She nods but then shakes her head as the tears fall.

"I watched; I watched the whole thing...I-I'm a monster! How could I do that?"

He shakes his head. "No, you did what you had to do to protect this pack, you did the right thing. I'm proud of you, sweetheart. You saved my life; I could have lost everything if you hadn't done what you did."

She gives him a small smile. "I couldn't let him cheat and win. I knew Penelope would be able to use our powers wisely."

*P: I mean I could have killed him **less** violently but...whatever..."*

Penelope shrugs her shoulders.

Т he entire crowd erupts in cheers as they now recognize the ruckus around them as he pulls her up.

He winces in pain as the bite is still healing.

"I think the steroids had traces of wolfsbane in them, I'm not healing as fast as I should."

He is still covered in blood and limping when he leans against her for balance and she holds him up until Evan gets there and takes over.

"Then we need to go to the pack doctor now."

He places his hand to her stomach. "And you need to get checked out too, who knows what exerting that amount of energy did to the baby, so I'll go if you do. That's the deal."

She sighs and rolls her eyes as they head toward the infirmary. Brent and Miles are being treated for the poisoning when they walk in. They seem okay despite what they went through and have no long-term effects. They bow their heads in respect and Kayd mouths a "Thank you" to his men for all they did to protect her today.

A doctor runs up to them, bowing quickly, "Alpha! Luna! Follow me please, I will examine you in the family room just over here." He ushers them into a quiet examination room.

He tends to Kayd's bite wound. Because he's not healing as he should, he pours rubbing alcohol on to disinfect it. Kayd immediately hisses and flips over a tray of medical equipment next to him with a roar.

"Honey please... let's not destroy the doctor's office."

He kisses her hand. "It stung and I reacted, my apologies doctor."

The doctor waves it off. "It's nothing Alpha, you've done much worse before..." He trails off as she looks at him like a scolded child.

"It's not what you think."

The doctor continues stitching him up and bandages his shoulder, wrapping around his upper chest.

"You were correct, the steroids he was taking were laced with wolfsbane, it is supposed to enhance results by making the body react to how poisonous wolfsbane is, then the body absorbs the steroids better. Shouldn't take more than a day to heal, just take it easy, sir."

The doctor bows as he leaves. A female doctor comes in, she's reviewing the clipboard before she makes eye contact and bows.

"Luna, I am Dr. Marrow, and I will be examining you to check the progress of your pregnancy. After today's events, I just want to make sure that everything is going as planned."

She instructs Kam to lie down and she squeezes some cold gel that causes her to jump. She smooths it over her entire abdomen before reaching for the ultrasound machine.

A few clicks and button pushes and the machine comes to life. She glides the wand over her abdomen and turns up the volume. What came out sounded like ocean waves or sonar.

After a few quiet yet intense moments the doctor sighs and turns to the parents to be.

"Well, doctor don't keep us waiting, is he or she okay?" Her hands are in his as they anticipate the news. He kisses her hand to relax her, but it doesn't seem to work this time.

Right before the doctor tells them there is a knock and Nessa peeks through the door.

"Hey, can we come in?"

Kayd nods and in walks Nessa, both of their mothers, and his command.

Kam looks at the doctor. "It's okay, they were going to barge in, regardless. Continue, please."

Dr. Marrow nods, "Well, everything is coming along just great, vitals are good, and mommy seems to be getting everything she needs right now and there seems to be no effect from the actions earlier. So, to answer your question, yes, he AND she are both okay...delivery will be in about three and a half months. Alpha, Luna."

The doctor smiles and nods as she takes her chart and walks out.

A gasp from her and then silence. Kam's tears flowed freely before she looked at Kayd, his hand covering her gel covered stomach and his tears start.

"Twins, baby doll did you hear, we're having twins..."

She nods and he kisses her ever so gently as they bask in the glorious news.

Later at home, Kayd covers her eyes and guides her up the stairs. "Babe, where are you taking me? I'm sure it's somewhere I've already been, and I don't trust myself not tripping and falling on these stairs."

He laughs and scoops her up and heads up the rest of the stairs. He covers her eyes the moment he sets her down.

"You have been to most places on our floor except the room closest to our bedroom, haven't you always wondered what was in there?"

With his hand still covering her view she just smiles and shrugs.

"I figured when it was time you'd tell or show me."

He turns her to him and her eyes open before he leans down and places the sweetest kiss to hers.

"Baby doll, my home is yours, every inch of it and yes I am glad you never looked because I wanted to see your face when I revealed it to you. I've always dreamed of a day where I would have a wife and a family and because of you I do, I have my beautiful girl who fights for me because our love is undeniable. And now, you carry our babies...twins, I still can't believe it! Guess, though I'm revealing it to you now, I'll have to remodel for two..."

She hears the click of the door handle before he ushers her inside, keeping her eyes covered.

She inhales deeply. "It smells like lavender and vanilla."

"Your senses are super sensitive but yeah, I read it's calming and soothing to babies and their mother."

He drops his hands and her eyes automatically open to the most beautiful nursery. She takes in all the details and she couldn't help but get emotional.

"Oh baby, it's...it's perfect. Well, perfect for one baby now we have to add another crib and another chair but other than that, it's beautiful, I love it!"

She grazes her finger across the soft chenille blanket hanging from the crib. "How long have you had this set up?"

He sits on the window nook facing the forest. "Way before you my dearest...I had a vision of this, it's just that I didn't have the key piece, my mate. I knew exactly how I wanted it to look and what would be in it. I would watch her as she cradles our baby while sitting in the rocker, humming a nursery rhyme. It was the most beautiful vision ever. Honestly, people thought I was crazy putting together a room with no one even in my life, but I knew she would come, I knew you would come."

She rubs her stomach as she slides her arms around his waist, and he does the same.

"You didn't have me, but you do now, and we are about to be parents, even through all the John/Bridget drama we still came out on top. You are my King and I, your Queen and soon to be your wife." He smiles looking down at her.

"Our love story should be written..."

She rubs her belly. "Yeah, but who would believe it?" They share a laugh as they exit the nursery through the door that leads to their bedroom.

(Six months later)

"O h, you have got to be kidding me!

UGH...I-I I can't do this I just need a breather..."
Kam sits on the window nook breathing heavily.
She straightens her garter before she huffs and
stands back up. "Okay, let's get this dress on."
Nessa and her mother's maneuver the sheer long
sleeved white lace gown over her body, it was a
mermaid style with an open back, the lace detail
was stunning throughout the dress and was covered
in Swarovski crystals.

She looked like a princess. Yes, she was a Queen,
but every girl dreamed of being a princess at their
wedding.

Instead of a traditional veil, they added clipped lace
to her crown which cascaded down her back
perfectly. Her natural curls fall perfectly to frame
her face. When she turned to the mirror, she was
absolutely stunned at how beautiful she looked. Her
tears fell but she caught them in the embroidered
handkerchief that her father had especially made for
this occasion, bearing the mark of her pack and the
mark of the Legacies.

Nessa sits her down to start her makeup. "Okay my
dearest best friend, let's get these tears out of the
way so I can make you look as gorgeous as you do

in this dress. I am going to make his jaw drop when he sees you." Kam's leg shakes incessantly. "Kammi bear, I can't do your makeup if you don't calm down! Sheesh, it's just like the Luna ceremony."

Kam turns around instantly. "But it's not Nessa, this is the ceremony where we confess our love in front of friends and family, where we are bound by our words for all to witness. This is what I've dreamed about since I was twelve and here we are. It's so much different from what I imagined, the circumstances are something I could never imagine, we're talking werewolves, magic, and all sorts of fairy tales but that is now a part of my life."

Her mother takes her hand. "It is dear, but it is those differences that make your bond stronger. I remember when your father and I got married, my word, I thought I was going to pass out but the moment those chapel doors opened and I met his gaze, I knew everything was perfect. Don't focus on anything else but Kayden and you'll know. I love you, my beautiful girl." She kisses her daughter on the forehead. "Thank you, mom. You're right, I can't wait to marry the man of my dreams."

Kayd stands at the altar looking handsome in his cobalt blue smoker's jacket with black lapels and black pants. His groomsmen wore solid cobalt blue suits and black ties, Kayd wore no tie. He looks out at the 100 or so guests and sighs. "This is more nerve-wracking than the Luna ceremony! And there's only a hundred people here, not 700."

Evan steps in front of the nervous groom and straightens him up. "While the Luna ceremony is important, it is required but a wedding is an intimate confession of love, spending precious hours writing down your admiration for her, making sure every syllable emphasizes just how much you love her. We get it, we all do, we all went through this but now you have us supporting you and not as our Alpha, but as our brother. The words you profess today are only going to make her fall in love with you more, I promise." Evan looks him over and smiles while clapping his back. "You ready?" Kayd inhales deeply letting out his breath slowly. "More than ready to see my wife."

Kam and Kayd's mother stand in front of her. "We both have a gift for you. Your mother has the 'something old' and I have the 'something blue'. My Kayden is lucky to have found such a beautiful soul in you and I'm glad to have a daughter I adore and my precious grand babies. Anyways, before I cry again, here. It is a blue sapphire bracelet that I had today's date engraved with both of your initials so you can always remember this day when you two became one. I hope you like it." She clips it on her wrist and she is amazed by the deep-sea blue. She whispers a thank you fearing the tears will fall.

Her mother steps up with a smile. "My beautiful baby girl, this belonged to me and every day I was away from you I would look at it to remind me of the loves of my life and I want you to do the same." She places the silver locket on her daughter and opens it for her to see. On one side were her and her parents when she was a baby and the other side were her grandparents. "Oh mom, it's so beautiful. My family...I'll cherish this forever, thank you." Her mom gives her an air kiss to maintain her makeup.

There was a knock on the door and in walks Dina, their nanny. "Oh Luna, you look simply breathtaking. I brought the children so you could approve their outfits." Dina and another daycare worker bring in the twins. Kamden was handsomely dressed in his tiny black suit and Kayari was in a floral dress and matching headband. "Oh, they are just so cute! Mommy loves you so much. Now, tell me they have backup outfits just in case." She nods. Not to take any chances she gives each of them a kiss on the forehead. "Okay go before I start crying again." She blows her babies kisses as they head to their seats up front.

Kamden and Kayari came bursting into this world without any warning, in fact Kayd had to drive back from their date to get her to the infirmary. "Slow down, sweetheart, we have plenty of time, my water just broke." But that was not true because not one hour after making it to the nurses' station did Kayari make her debut with Kamden arriving five minutes later.

Kamari closes her eyes and inhales deeply then
there's another knock at the door. "Come in." Her
father walks in and he instantly starts to cry. "Oh,
my baby you look like an angel on earth. It's time..."
Nessa hands her the bouquet of white and blue
roses. She looks in the mirror and smiles. "Goodbye
Ms. Lee..."

The waiting was torture for Kayd, he felt all his
senses on high alert but then he caught a whiff of
her scent. She was on the other side of the doors and
his heart was pounding, which was clear to his best
man. "Hey, breathe...just breathe."

The music plays and her dad smiles. "Here we go..."

The white double lattice doors open and the crowd
gasps. Kam's eyes lock on Kayd. "Oh my god..."
she felt the lump in her throat while she fought back
the tears. "Sweet moon goddess there she is..." He
stumbles upon his words.
When they make their way to the altar her dad
pecks her on the cheek.

"You'll always be my baby girl."

"Thank you, daddy."

Kayd takes her hand, clutching his chest with the
other.
"Wow, baby doll you stole my breath as well as my
heart." She nods as they stand in front of the priest.

"And now we will let the bride and groom exchange vows. Kamari, please. "

She clears her throat and smiles slightly while trying to hold the dam of tears.

"Kayden, there are no words that fulfill how much I truly love you. Ever since you brought me into your world, I have felt safe, I have felt whole. Being the pack Luna has been the most fulfilling part of my life next to being a mother and I have you to thank for it all. From the moment you found me you have been nothing but compassionate and loving, getting through the difficult times and just loving me as I am and for that, thank you. My heart belongs to you, baby. I am bound to you; I love you Kayden James Miller."

His eyes filled with tears and she takes her handkerchief and wipes his tears. He takes a deep breath.

"Kamari, my light and my life. The moment I saw you I knew you were made for me. How could I ever be blessed with such a beautiful and kind soul? The woman who made me a father to the most beautiful children on this Earth, my legacy will pass on through them and for that I thank you. Every day we spend together I will spend showing you how much I love you, how much I cherish you, and how blessed I am to have you. You are my world Kamari Lee, don't ever forget it. I love you, baby doll."
Evan pats him on the back making him smile. He doesn't take his gaze off her, but he lets the tears fall freely.

"Alpha, you may now kiss your bride!"

Kayd dips her quickly, placing his lips gently on hers. "You have no idea how long I have waited to do that." She blushes. "Umm, since this morning?" And he shakes his head. "My whole life...thank you so much Mrs. Miller for loving me." He pulls her up from the kiss and they are unaware of the loud cheering surrounding them. "Thank you, Mr. Miller, for teaching me the true meaning of love. I love you so much." She squeezes his hand as she picks up Kayari and he picks up Kamden and they walk back down the aisle...happily ever after.

The End

www.ingramcontent.com/pod-product-compliance
Lightning Source LLC
Chambersburg PA
CBHW022110240626
47153CB00007B/2311